3 0132 01

D1758104

CALL OF THE SEA

Everything is going well for Cassie Lewis, working in her parents' boatyard in Devon with her children Tom and Lara. The boatyard is busy and sponsorship for her son Tom's round-the-world race is coming in. But dark clouds are on the horizon ... Cassie is unsure about her friendship with wealthy businessman Doug Hampshire. And as for James White, the harbour master, he's already fallen in love with her — but is she ready for anything more complicated?

JENNIFER BOHNET

CALL OF
THE SEA

Complete and Unabridged

LINFORD
Leicester

First published in Great Britain in 2004

First Linford Edition
published 2006

British Library CIP Data

Bohnet, Jennifer
    Call of the sea.—Large print ed.—
Linford romance library
    1. Single mothers—Fiction 2. Boatyards
—Fiction 3. Yachting—Fiction 4. Devon
(England)—Fiction 5. Love stories
6. Large type books
    I. Title
    823.9'2 [F]

    ISBN 1–84617–562–3

Published by
F. A. Thorpe (Publishing)
Anstey, Leicestershire

Set by Words & Graphics Ltd.
Anstey, Leicestershire
Printed and bound in Great Britain by
T. J. International Ltd., Padstow, Cornwall

1

'A Dangerous Business'

'And now here is the shipping forecast for sea areas . . . ' Cassie Lewis lay in bed early on Monday morning, listening to the measured tones of the announcer. Sleepily, she waited for the forecast for the area where her son, Tom, was currently sailing.

' . . . Biscay. Gale force seven rising to eight or nine.'

In an instant, Cassie was awake and out of bed. Gales were not good. Tom needed some wind and rough seas on these trials, but too much could be dangerous.

Dressing quickly in jeans and sweater, Cassie made her way quietly downstairs. Lara's bedroom door was slightly ajar and she could just glimpse the hump that represented her sleeping daughter snuggled under the duvet.

From habit, Cassie glanced out of the kitchen window as she filled the kettle, but it was still too dark to see much.

A few lights were showing in the cottages on the hillside and the occasional masthead light was visible on boats at anchor in the middle of the river, but it was the moon which lit the river and outlined the twelfth-century castle that stood protectively at the mouth of the estuary.

From the marina directly outside her open kitchen window, Cassie could hear the gentle twanging of mast stays as yachts moved with the incoming tide.

A light was shining in the boatyard and Cassie guessed her father was making his customary early start to the day. She hesitated before reaching for an extra mug.

She needed to talk to him. Perhaps now would be a good time. She'd take him a cup of tea in any case.

'Morning, Dad.'

Bill Holdsworth looked up from the piece of wood he was planing.

'Well, you're an early bird and no mistake. Couldn't you sleep?'

Cassie shook her head.

'Bad forecast for Biscay,' she explained briefly.

'I heard. Reckon we'll get the tail end of it in about forty-eight hours. Still, Tom should make good time coming home.'

Taking the mug of tea, Bill glanced at his only daughter. She was clearly worrying about something.

'You all right?' he asked. When Cassie didn't answer immediately he went on quietly. 'Not a good year for young Tom to be doing this race, is it?'

Cassie's shoulders slumped.

'No, it's not. Do you realise it's twenty years since Miles died? The anniversary is while Tom's away racing.'

Bill looked at his daughter, a gentle compassion filling his eyes. He was so proud of the way she'd coped with being widowed so young. Tom and Lara were a real credit to her. And encouraging them both to take up sailing when they'd shown an interest couldn't have been easy.

'It's different these days,' Bill said, finally breaking the silence. 'It's still a dangerous business — I'm not saying otherwise. But what with hi-tech navigation and satellite phones, it's safer than it's ever been. The boats are built differently, too. They're a lot stronger.

'I reckon if Miles had been sailing today he'd have been OK — just like Tom will be,' he said confidently.

'Oh, Dad, I couldn't bear it if anything happened to him.'

'Nothing's going to happen to him, lass. He's a good sailor. He's going to bring credit to us all by taking *Holdsworth's Clotted Cream* around the world and bringing her home safely.'

Cassie smiled weakly at her father. She'd known she could rely on him to talk sense. Perhaps now was the moment to ask him about . . . but Bill was already speaking again.

'Mind you, we could do with a few more sponsors. Any news on that front?'

'We're hoping to hear from a couple of firms today.'

'Good. And don't forget, Dexter Munro is waiting for Tom's final confirmation as soon as he gets back from these trials.'

'I won't. Oh, and while I remember, could you tell Mum I won't be around for lunch today? I've got an appointment with the bank and I thought I'd do a bit of shopping afterwards.'

Bill looked momentarily worried.

'The bank?'

'Don't worry, it's not a problem. I want to talk to them about sponsorship. Right, I'd better get back. There's a lot to do. I'll e-mail Tom before I go out. You'll be here to take his midday call?'

Bill nodded.

'I wouldn't miss it.'

Tragedy

Making her way across the yard back to her small house, converted out of what had previously been a warehouse, Cassie found herself wondering, not for the first time, what her life would have been like if Miles had lived.

He'd been en route to Cape Town in a single-handed race that he'd been so confident of winning when he'd been lost overboard.

'I'm on a roll,' he'd said. 'I've just won the Round Britain. This is my year.'

But it had all ended in tragedy when Miles and his boat had disappeared somewhere off the Azores during a storm.

If Miles had survived the race, they'd planned to base themselves in France, down on the Côte d'Azur near Antibes, and establish some sort of sailing business.

Instead, Cassie had found herself heading home to the West Country with two small children, a widow at twenty-nine.

Naturally, her parents had been supportive, and slowly Cassie and the children had recovered from the trauma of Miles's death. Within six months of returning home, Cassie was once again working in the family business, helping her parents to expand it, and slowly rebuilding her own life.

It wasn't how she'd envisaged her life turning out, but she'd been happy enough with her children, living back in the security of her own family.

Just recently, though, she'd found herself feeling as if she'd never left home. If it weren't for Tom and Lara, who were the living proof of her marriage, she might sometimes have found it hard to believe her seven years with Miles had ever been.

Over time, the memories of that short period in her life had taken on the sepia-like quality of a much-loved photograph.

Tom, just five when his father died,

said he'd only one memory of him — not sailing, but playing football with him in the small garden of their house. Lara had no memory of her father at all, a fact which Cassie knew upset her daughter.

Memories or not, both children had Miles's physical features, and Tom, at 6′ 3″, had also inherited his height. And there was no doubt whom they both took after when it came to sailing.

For six years now, Tom, as well as being involved in the family business, had been pursuing a career as a professional yachtsman. Cassie was very proud of his achievements. According to Tom, this round-the-world race would set the seal on it.

'In another four years, when the next one is held, Mai and I will probably have a family.' He'd hesitated, clearly choosing his next words with care.

'I wouldn't want to put myself in the position where I might do to Mai and our children what Dad did to us.'

Cassie had struggled to fight back the

tears at his words.

As she let herself back into the house, she realised she hadn't discussed with her father the matter she'd intended. The moment hadn't been right after all.

Lara was in the kitchen, leaning sleepily against the Aga rail, her hands clasped around a mug of coffee.

'Morning, Mum. Coffee's in the pot if you want one.'

'What are you up to today?' Cassie asked as she poured herself a coffee.

'Mai and I are still trying to get the main cabin on the barge finished. We're almost there. We've just got the portholes to paint and the curtains to hang, then we can start on the galley.'

Over the years Bill Holdsworth had expanded his initial boat-building yard into a real family concern.

Cassie had taken over the day-to-day running of the yacht chandlery and these days was learning more about the book-keeping side of the business from her mother. Now in her seventies, Liz Holdsworth was pleased to have some time to pursue other interests.

The marina side of the business was run by Cassie's brother, Rufus, and his wife, Bridget. The barge was to be Tom and Mai's project. Lara was giving them a helping hand for a year until she decided what she was going to do with her life.

'The business needs to expand, Gramps, if it's to survive and support us all,' Tom had said. 'We can use the barge as a base for a sailing school and offer accommodation as well.'

The 100 ft barge, abandoned in the Isle of Wight, had been bought for a song and towed slowly down channel. For the last couple of weeks it had been tied up alongside the Holdsworth pontoon, waiting to be allocated a permanent mooring by the Harbour Commission.

Once the boatyard men had done some essential maintenance on it, Mai and Lara had spent hours decorating and generally sprucing it up in readiness for its first season.

'If you're going into town today, Mum, could you pop into the printers and pick up the brochures? We'll have to mail them out soon,' Lara said.

'Yes, OK. Anything else you want whilst I'm there? Will you be home for dinner this evening?'

Lara shook her head.

'No, thanks. Sebastian's booked a table at Le Bistro. He wants us to have a special evening together before he reports for duty on Thursday.'

'Le Bistro really is special,' Cassie said. 'Very swish.'

'Hmm. I think he plans on proposing to me tonight,' Lara said quietly.

Cassie felt her heart skip a beat in trepidation, but before she could say anything Lara was on her way out.

'Right, I'm off to the barge,' her daughter said. 'See you later.' And she was gone, the kitchen door closing quickly behind her.

Cassie sighed. She'd wanted to ask Lara what she planned to say if Lieutenant Sebastian Grove did propose.

11

Best Friends

The phone was ringing as Cassie walked into her office behind the chandlery store an hour or so later.

'Cassie? It's Anna.'

'Hi. Lovely to hear from you. How are you?'

'OK — well, sort of. Can I come and stay for a while?'

'Of course. When?'

'Wednesday?'

'Fine.'

They chatted for a few moments before saying goodbye, both looking forward to the forthcoming visit.

Anna and Cassie had been best friends since primary school days. Anna had moved away when she got married and had spent the last twenty-five years living and farming in Wales. Letters, lots of telephone calls and yearly visits had kept them in touch.

When Anna's husband had died five years ago, Cassie had tried to persuade her friend to come home, but Anna had refused. She was going to stay and help her son, David, to run the farm.

Since then, visits had been few and far between. Cassie wondered how long Anna would be able to stay this time.

Switching on the computer and logging on, Cassie checked her e-mails and heaved a sigh of relief. There was finally one from Rule of Thumb Technology, confirming its offer of sponsorship and naming a sum of money that would certainly ease Tom's current cash flow problems.

No news from the other major sponsor she was waiting to hear from, though. Time was running out on that one.

E-mailing Tom, she told him the good news regarding Rule of Thumb, said how much she was looking forward to seeing him in three or four days' time, and wished him a safe journey home.

The next couple of hours flew by as Cassie made phone calls and sent faxes and e-mails on Tom's behalf. Finding sponsorship and organising things for him was rapidly becoming a full-time job, and she still had all the day-to-day jobs to do for the chandlery as well as the accounts for the yard.

It was midday before she was finished and she realised she was going to have to get a move on if she wasn't to be late for her appointment at the bank.

Holdsworth Boatyard & Marina, although only a mile up river from town by boat, was a three-mile drive by car along winding Devonshire lanes.

Most of the time, trips into town were made using the small river launch, but today Cassie opted to take her car. She didn't want to look too windswept for her appointment.

His usual pleasant courteous self, Mr Hollis, the bank manager, greeted her warmly.

'Although I'm afraid I don't have an official answer for you yet, Mrs Lewis, the good news is that Head Office is still considering your sponsorship package.

'Hopefully, by this time next week, I'll have a definite favourable decision. I'll ring you as soon as I hear anything.'

Leaving the bank, Cassie made her way to the printers and collected the barge brochures. As she passed the Harbour Commission offices, James White came striding out and relieved her of the parcel.

'Cassie, how lovely to see you! Let me carry that. Have you time to have lunch with me?'

The moment she agreed, Cassie found herself being steered in the direction of the Riverside Café.

All She Wanted

Once seated at a window table with panoramic views of the harbour and the river mouth, she smiled at James.

'This is an unexpected treat.'

'We should do it more often,' he said. 'Make it a regular date.'

Cassie smiled back but said nothing.

It was a long time since she'd had a regular date.

James looked at Cassie, wondering if she realised what an attractive woman she was. Ever since he'd arrived in town as the newly-appointed Harbour Master a year ago, he'd been fascinated by her.

Although she'd accepted his invitation to the cinema once or twice, he was still no closer to touching her heart. She'd told him on their first outing that she was happy to be friends, but that was all she wanted — friendship.

Recently he'd begun to suspect that, despite being surrounded by family, she was as lonely as he'd been since his wife died eight years ago. But getting past the barrier she'd built around herself was proving far more difficult than he'd ever envisaged.

Now, sitting opposite her, he entertained her with tales of his life among the men who formed the Harbour Committee and were, in effect, his bosses.

'Honestly, Cassie, I don't think there's a man amongst them who remembers the freedom a boat gives you.

'Come sailing with me on Saturday?' he asked suddenly.

The pain that surged through her body at his question was as unexpected as it was hurtful.

'I can't,' she answered, frantically trying to think of an excuse. 'Tom is due home at the end of the week. I must be there for him,' she said finally, not meeting James's eyes.

Like Tom and Lara, Cassie had loved sailing in her youth. She'd lived for the exhilaration of skimming over the waves, the mainsail billowing in the wind, the freedom James had referred to of being out on the water.

Sailing had given her Miles. They'd met on a RYA training course. But sailing had taken Miles away from her. From then on, the sport had lost its personal magic for her.

When Tom and Lara took up the

pursuit, she'd forced herself to go with them for safety reasons. She'd even sailed with them up river to Miles's favourite picnic spot in an effort to keep his memory alive for them, and herself.

But for years now, since they'd been old enough to sail on their own, she hadn't set foot in a sailing dinghy or yacht.

She didn't have a problem using the motor launch on the river. It was just a mode of transport that helped her do her job.

But sailing was something that belonged most definitely to Miles and her past.

Now, James, watching her intently, was about to say something, but changed his mind when he saw her expression.

'OK, no sailing,' he said instead. 'How about dinner and the theatre on Saturday evening? Even if Tom is home, won't he and Mai want to be together? They haven't been married long, have they?'

'Three months. And you're right. They will need some time on their own. Dinner and theatre it is, then. Thank you.'

As she accepted James's invitation, Cassie inwardly chided herself for not realising that she'd have to get used to not coming first in Tom's world, now that he had Mai.

Sebastian's Plans

Lara dressed with extra care for her date with Sebastian that evening. The proposal of marriage from the man you love is a moment that's supposed to stay with you for ever. She wanted to be able to look back and remember it as perfect.

Mai had gently teased her that afternoon, when Lara had mentioned her suspicions about Sebastian's plans.

'It doesn't matter where the proposal is made or how you look. It's the fact that you love the man who is proposing.'

'Where did Tom pop the question?'

Mai laughed.

'Oh, it was totally unromantic! I was hanging upside down, cleaning the bilge of an old boat. I was filthy, wet and smelled terrible. Tom said he had this sudden urge to take me away from it all.'

She glanced around the barge and giggled.

'He didn't take me far, though, did he?'

'How did you know you wanted to marry him? How could you be sure that he really was the one?' Lara asked seriously.

'I just knew. I love him and couldn't bear the thought of him not being in my life,' Mai said simply. 'When he's away I worry constantly and I miss him terribly.'

She hesitated, looking thoughtfully at Lara before going on.

'If you have any doubts, say no. And remember it's not just Sebastian you'd be marrying, but in his case, the Navy as well. It's a different way of life.

'Anyway, I thought you had plans of your own to do some more professional sailing?'

There was a short silence before Lara answered.

'I did. I do.'

'Well, how will that fit in with Sebastian and the Navy?'

'He loves sailing, too,' Lara said quickly. 'He wants his own boat.' She paused. 'But he thinks it's just a hobby for me — not a career option.'

Mai looked at her.

'Surely that's for you to decide, not him?'

Lara shrugged her shoulders.

'Lack of sponsorship will probably do the deciding for me.'

Now, as she put on her amber earrings, she thought about their conversation.

She was in love with Sebastian, there was no doubt about that. He was so handsome and charming and her heart quickened at the sight of him. But did she want to spend the rest of her life with him?

She didn't feel the way Mai did about Tom. She was looking forward to some time on her own whilst Sebastian was away on his latest posting!

It was ages since she'd had a proper sail in *It's Mine!,* her battered 25ft sailing yacht.

She always seemed to be too busy these days. Her time seemed to be taken up either with work or with Sebastian and the various functions he wanted her to attend with him — functions that she knew would only increase once she was a Naval wife.

Mai had clearly been happy to give up the lifestyle she'd carved out for herself and throw her lot in with Tom and his ambitions.

Lara sighed. Would Sebastian expect her to do the same once she was Mrs Grove? Would her own desires have to be sacrificed for his? More importantly, was she prepared to make the sacrifice?

She and Tom were planning to compete together in next year's Round the Islands race and, if she could raise the money, she dreamed of being the next Ellen MacArthur and sailing around the world single-handed.

But with the next Vendée Globe just four years away, so far nobody she'd approached had shown a flicker of interest in sponsoring her.

Picking up her bag, she went downstairs to wait for Sebastian. Cassie and Mai were in the kitchen, poring over a large sea chart.

Lara recognised it instantly as a chart of the Southern Ocean — an ocean that would play a large part in Tom's life in the coming months.

'We're trying to work out some alternatives for Tom,' Mai said. 'But, in the end, it will clearly depend on the prevalent weather.'

Just as Lara had leaned over to take a closer look, a car tooted outside.

'That'll be Sebastian,' she observed. 'I'm off. Don't wait up, Mum.' And Lara was gone.

Mai and Cassie looked at each other. 'Do you think she will . . . ?' They both asked the question together before laughing wryly.

'Oh, Mai, I do hope not,' Cassie admitted. 'I like Sebastian well enough, but I'm not sure he's the right man for Lara.' She sighed. 'I wish Tom was home. She listens to him more than me. He'd stop her doing anything foolish.'

'A few more days and he will be. And if she does get engaged tonight . . . well, engagements can always be broken, can't they?'

Cassie smiled affectionately at her daughter-in-law, feeling comforted. Tom had certainly made a wise choice when he'd married Mai.

'Have you thought any more about staying on here when Tom gets home rather than moving back to River View?' Cassie asked.

The small cottage where Tom and Mai had been living since their marriage was just a hundred yards along the riverbank from the boatyard.

Mai shook her head.

'When Tom is away I'm glad of the

company down here, but when he's home, well . . . ' She smiled shyly at Cassie.

'It's nice to be on our own — especially as Tom is going to be away for months soon. I'll certainly be back then, if I may.'

'Sudden Decision'

Cassie and Anna sat sipping a glass of wine, waiting for their lasagne.

Even early on a Wednesday evening, the bistro, tucked away in a quiet street behind the harbour, was already busy.

Anna had insisted on them eating out.

'I don't want to dress up, so nowhere posh — just somewhere we can sit and catch up on the gossip without interruptions.

'Oh, and please may we go by launch? It's ages since I've been out on the river. I want to take in deep gulps of sea air and blow all the cobwebs away.'

Cassie had laughed at that, remembering how much Anna had hated fresh air when they were growing up.

'What's the news from Tom?'

'He expects to be off Land's End some time late tomorrow. So, fingers crossed, he should be home on Friday afternoon,' Cassie said.

'When does the race itself start?'

'Six weeks on Sunday. Will you still be here? I warn you, though, the next few weeks will be hectic. If you're around, you'll get roped in.'

'I'm not going back,' Anna announced.

'Never?' Cassie was astonished.

Anna shook her head.

'I'll have to collect my things, of course, and tie up some loose ends, but otherwise, no. I'm going to find somewhere down here to live.'

'Why the sudden decision?'

'I've been thinking about it for ages and now David has officially taken over the farm, I'm free to do my own thing. And I want to come back.'

'Are you sure? When Harry died I

asked if you were going to come home and you were emphatic your place was with the farm. What's really changed?'

'Foot and mouth,' Anna said quietly. 'For hundreds of farmers it killed more than the livestock. It certainly destroyed my spirit. Harry and I put so much of ourselves into the farm; I simply can't face doing it all again without him.

'David is resilient and young enough to cope, but I'm not. So I'm coming back to my roots.'

Cassie was silent for a moment.

'Well, I wish it was for any other reason, but I'm so pleased to have you back,' she said finally. 'And until you find somewhere you like, the spare room is yours. No arguments.'

'Thanks, Cassie,' Anna said gratefully. 'Now, you haven't mentioned my god-daughter yet. What's Lara up to these days?'

'Can you believe she's considering a proposal of marriage?' Cassie said. 'And also getting extremely frustrated at not being taken seriously by race organisers and sponsors.'

'Who's the boyfriend? The one I met last time — Sebastian something? Very good-looking Naval officer?'

Cassie nodded.

'That's the one. He asked her on Monday and apparently she's agreed to think about it whilst he's away on a tour of duty.'

'Hmm. He's quite a catch — though I can't see Lara as a Navy wife, somehow,' Anna said. 'She likes doing her own thing, doesn't she? Besides, what about her sailing?'

'Old Fashioned'

Cassie sighed.

'She can't find enough sponsorship to do much at the moment. She's helping with the barge and when Tom gets back she'll work with him on preparing *Clotted Cream* for the single-handed.

28

'I think she's crewing in a couple of races later in the season, but I also know Sebastian is putting pressure on her to give it all up.'

Anna pulled a face.

'That's a bit old-fashioned, isn't it?'

Cassie agreed.

'If Lara can find some sponsorship and can prove herself as a yachts-woman, I reckon she'll carry on racing whatever Sebastian says. But,' and she shook her head, 'if not, I'm afraid she'll end up just getting married.'

'Lara's got too much spirit simply to give in.' Anna said confidently. 'Besides, the fact that she's considering the proposal makes me pretty sure she'll turn him down. I didn't have to think twice when Harry proposed. Did you when Miles . . . ?'

'No. If he hadn't, I was going to propose to him on February twenty-ninth.' Cassie smiled, remembering how much she'd wanted to marry Miles.

'Perhaps you're right,' she went on.

'Having to think about it must mean she's not sure. What a dilemma — settling down or sailing the high seas. I'll worry whatever she decides.' Cassie grinned ruefully before finishing her wine.

Wandering through town later, Anna stopped outside the estate agency and took one of the free advertising papers out of a rack.

'Bedtime reading,' she said, stuffing it into her bag.

'I think we'd better be heading back,' Cassie said. 'The wind's gusting and the tide will be on the turn soon.'

Anxious

In fact they were lucky to make it home before thirty-six hours of bad weather set in. As Bill had predicted, they were suffering the tail end of the storm from Biscay.

The next day, as the gale raged outside, Cassie worked in the office, clearing paperwork so that she could devote as much time as possible to Tom's preparation over the following few weeks.

Lara and Mai roped Anna in to help with finishing the barge. In the evening the four of them sat around the large wooden table in Cassie's kitchen, drinking coffee and stuffing the barge brochures into envelopes ready for posting.

Although nobody said anything, everybody was anxious to keep their minds off the bad weather Tom would be experiencing on his way home.

Late on Thursday evening, Mai got an e-mail from him saying he was in the Channel and hoped to be home within twelve hours. Everybody breathed a collective sigh of relief and went to bed, happy in the knowledge that Tom and *Clotted Cream* were almost home.

It was midday Friday before *Clotted Cream* was sighted. James rang Cassie to give her the welcome news.

'I've just been out to give Tom my

official routine check and he's now on his way up river to you. He said he hasn't slept for forty-one hours because of the weather. He looks all in, but everything else is fine.'

'Thanks, James. I'll see you tomorrow night.'

Cassie replaced the receiver and went down to the barge to find Mai and Lara. Together, they waited on the landing slip and watched as Tom negotiated his way to *Clotted Cream's* berth.

At last the yacht was secured and Tom waved as he clambered into the launch for the short journey to shore.

Over sandwiches and coffee he told them a little about the sea trials.

'It's all in the log, but basically we're going to have to do some work on the hydraulic pulleys. And the self-steering gear wants some fine-tuning. Other than that, it's a question of checking her over, provisioning her for the first leg and getting her round to Plymouth for the start.'

Cassie looked at him. A week's growth of stubble covered his chin; his favourite Guernsey sweater showed signs of having been lived in for several days and his hands looked sore and weather-beaten. But despite his obvious tiredness his enthusiasm still shone through.

Not for the first time, she was reminded of Miles. Single-minded determination definitely ran in the Lewis family.

'By the way, I had an e-mail from Dexter. He's coming to pick up my entry forms himself. We haven't got room in River View, Mum, so is it all right if he stays here for the night?'

'When's he coming?'

'Some time tomorrow.'

Cassie nodded. She'd always had an open house policy as far as Tom and Lara's friends were concerned.

'He hasn't been here before, has he?'

'No. It must be three years since I last saw him. We crewed together in the Fastnet, then he went off to America and became more involved in the business side of things. Pity, really. He's a good sailor and a nice bloke.' Tom stifled a yawn.

'I'm absolutely exhausted. Do you mind if Mai and I leave you all to it? We'll have a family conference over the week-end to sort out the final preparations, OK?'

Cassie stood by the kitchen door, watching as Tom and Mai walked hand in hand down the path. Lara was striding out in front of them.

'I like Mai,' Anna said unexpectedly. 'She and Tom are good together. But it's hard standing back, isn't it?' She gave Cassie an understanding look.

'Come on,' she continued, 'I'll give you a hand clearing up and then I'll show you the details of a house I'm considering.'

Twenty minutes later, Anna handed Cassie an estate agent's blurb.

'What do you think?'

Before Cassie could say anything, the kitchen door flew open and both women turned in surprise as Lara ran in.

'Mum! Phone 999! Tom's had an accident on the barge. We need an ambulance quickly.'

Unconscious

In fact it was the air ambulance that landed in the field at the river's edge and took Tom off to hospital, leaving Cassie shaken and not believing what had happened.

On the way home, Tom had decided to take a quick look at the work Mai and Lara had done on the barge. Used to the narrow steep steps leading down into *Clotted Cream's* hull, he'd apparently misjudged his footing as he'd turned to descend the barge's wider companionway. He'd made a grab for the handrail which disastrously gave way.

He'd fallen backwards down the flight of steps, ending in an unconscious crumpled heap at the bottom.

James arrived just as they were lifting

Tom into the helicopter and had a quick word with the crew before running across to Cassie.

She waited for him fearfully.

'Did they tell you anything?'

James shook his head.

'They want to get him to the General as quickly as possible. The hospital is already on standby to receive them.'

James had no intention of telling either Cassie or Mai what the paramedic on board had actually said about Tom's condition.

'Is Bill coming to the hospital with you?'

'No. He and Mum are staying with Lara. She's in a bit of a state.'

'I'll drive you and bring you back,' James said. 'Come on. We'll take my car.'

The forty-minute journey to the hospital seemed to take for ever. After an initial unsuccessful attempt to break the silence, James switched on the car radio, leaving Mai and Cassie to their own thoughts, and concentrated on his driving.

Casualty was crowded, but the senior nurse led them to an anteroom and said the doctor would be with them shortly.

'I'll go and find a coffee machine, shall I?' James offered.

'That would be nice. Black, no sugar, for both of us,' Cassie said, glancing at Mai who was perched on the edge of her seat, nervously twisting her wedding ring round and round. The doctor arrived just as James was passing round the thin polystyrene cups.

'Mrs Lewis?'

Both Cassie and Mai turned at the name, coffee forgotten.

'I'm Doctor Webster,' he said, talking to Mai. 'We're about to take Tom up to theatre. As far as we can tell at the moment, he's suffering from some internal bruising and both his legs are broken. Once he's been operated on, we'll move him into Intensive Care.'

He glanced at Cassie and then at Mai again.

'I'm afraid only one of you can see

him for five minutes before he goes to theatre.'

Mai was on her way out of the room instantly.

Cassie stopped the doctor as he went to follow her.

'He will be all right, won't he?'

'A lot depends on his internal bruising, and of course, it will be several months before he's walking again, but yes, hopefully he will make a full recovery.'

'When Can I See Him?'

The storm finally blew itself out during Friday night, and Saturday dawned calm and bright.

Anna was the first up and Cassie found her in the kitchen, busy organising breakfast.

'Just coffee for me. Any sign of Mai or Lara?' she asked.

Anna inclined her head in the direction of the boatyard.

'Lara's wandering around out there somewhere. She said something about giving *It's Mine!* a scrub to take her mind off things.

'I've taken Mai breakfast in bed and given her strict instructions to stay there. She looks terrible. You don't look good, either,' she added frankly.

Cassie ignored the comment.

'Do you think it's too early to phone the hospital?' she said instead.

'I'd give it another hour.'

Cassie drank her coffee and nibbled at the piece of toast Anna pushed across the table to her.

She'd always been terrified at the thought of something happening to Tom at sea, but had never dreamed an accident would happen on home territory.

'I can't wait an hour,' she said suddenly. 'I'm going to phone now.'

Anna watched her anxiously as she waited to be put through to Tom's ward and asked to speak to the nurse in charge.

'I'm Mrs Lewis, Tom's mother.

Could you tell me how he is, please? And when can I see him?' She listened attentively. 'I see. Thank you.'

Putting the phone down, she turned to Anna.

'He's as comfortable as can be expected. He's still quite heavily sedated.'

She turned as Lara opened the kitchen door.

'Morning, love. Are you all right? You look shattered.'

Lara nodded as she helped herself to a mug of coffee.

'I am. Do you think they'll let me see Tom, today?'

Cassie shook her head.

'Sorry, love. I've just phoned the hospital. Mai can go any time and I'm allowed five minutes this afternoon, but nobody else.'

The morning passed quicker than Cassie had expected. Both she and Mai were kept busy answering phone calls from people anxious to know how Tom was. News of the accident had certainly spread fast.

It was after one o'clock when Cassie, Mai and Anna finally set off for the hospital, Anna going along just to keep Cassie company on the drive back. Bill and Liz had volunteered to collect Mai when she was ready to come home.

Tom was semi-conscious as Cassie walked into the small ward, and he smiled weakly at her in greeting.

'Hi, Mum.'

Carefully, she leaned over and gave him a gentle kiss on his bruised face.

'Oh, Tom, it's good to see you. Mai's waiting outside but they said I could have five minutes first.'

Not wanting to tire Tom out before Mai got to his bedside, Cassie left before her time was up. To have seen her son and reassured herself that he would be all right was enough.

As Cassie and Anna got out of the car in the boatyard, they saw Lara walking slowly towards the house, accompanied by a tall man whom Cassie didn't recognise. A reporter perhaps, checking the story of Tom's accident?

She'd soon know. Lara had seen them and was bringing him over to meet her.

'Mum, this is Dexter Munro — Tom's friend. And race organiser,' she added as Cassie looked at her blankly.

The events of the last twenty-four hours had pushed everything out of her mind.

'I've told him about the accident.'

'Nice to meet you, Mrs Lewis. I can't tell you how sorry I am about Tom. Please give him my best wishes and let him know I'll be in touch. Do you have any idea yet how long he'll be out of action?'

'The doctor said several months.'

'So my visit today to collect the entry forms for the race is irrelevant, isn't it?' Dexter said slowly. 'There's no way Tom is going to be able to compete with *Clotted Cream* now.'

There was a short silence as they all looked at each other, realising the major consequence of Tom's accident.

'I've been thinking about that,' Lara said quietly. 'It's down to me, isn't it?'

Cassie, Dexter and Anna all turned to look at her.

'What do you mean?' Cassie said, knowing, even as she asked the question, exactly what Lara meant.

'I can do it instead of Tom,' Lara said determinedly.

Cassie started to protest.

'No, Lara, I don't think that's an answer.'

But Lara interrupted her.

'Why not? Just give me one good reason why I shouldn't enter *Clotted Cream* in the race instead of Tom?'

2

'It's In My Blood!'

The argument looked set to continue all weekend.

Lara's words, 'Just give me one good reason why I shouldn't enter *Clotted Cream* in the race instead of Tom?' had been met with stunned silence.

Cassie, clearly struggling to keep her emotions under control, had simply looked at her.

It was Dexter who finally spoke.

'I can think of one very good reason — lack of experience.'

Lara looked at him coldly.

'I am experienced. I've done lots of sailing, both as crew and as skipper. And I've done a single-handed.'

Dexter shrugged.

'I know you've competed in the Fastnet and I also know that you've done some single-handed sailing, Lara. Tom's always talking about his gutsy kid sister.

'But two or three weeks crossing the Atlantic alone is nothing compared to the dangers you'd face and the months you'd be away on this race. Besides, *Clotted Cream* is in a different league to the boats you've sailed alone before.'

'I know I can do it,' Lara said with determination. 'And this may be the only chance I get to prove myself. Besides, there's so much at stake. Gramps has invested a lot of money in helping Tom buy *Clotted Cream*. Some of the sponsors' money has already been spent on preparing the boat. If she doesn't compete, will we have to give it back?'

'If it's just a question of the boat being seen to compete, we can find a professional racing skipper to take her round,' Cassie had said. 'You don't have to do it.'

'The point is, Mum, I want to do it. I

want the names *Clotted Cream*, Holdsworth Boatyard and Lara Lewis to be up there with the winners. And, in case you've forgotten, competitive sailing is as much in my blood as it is in Tom's.'

'No, I haven't forgotten,' Cassie said quietly. 'But it doesn't mean that I have to stand by and say nothing while you overstretch yourself doing something that could be beyond your capabilities and is dangerous.'

'Perhaps I could take a look at the preparations you've already made? See how much more sponsorship you need,' Dexter asked unexpectedly.

'Can I trust you to be impartial?' Lara stared at him.

'I'm just trying to help here, Lara. It makes very little difference to me whether *Clotted Cream* takes part in the race or not — or who is her skipper.'

'Everything is in my office,' Cassie said. 'Why don't you take Dexter and go through all the paperwork with him, Lara? I'll see you both later.'

★ ★ ★

As she went through the paperwork with Dexter, Lara struggled to keep her thoughts focused on the race and not think about Tom lying in a hospital bed.

Dexter was certainly very efficient, going through files and grasping their contents quickly. He soon had several sheets of paper filled with figures.

'Everything's exceptionally business-like,' he observed. 'Is that your doing?'

Lara shook her head.

'No, I can't take the credit for that,' she admitted. 'It's Mum's department. She's extremely organised. I do more on the practical side. Most of my time's been spent working on the boat with Tom. I really do know her inside out.

'How are the finances looking?' she went on, indicating his sheaf of papers.

Dexter shrugged noncommittally.

'I'll have to run the figures through a calculator before I can tell for sure. Incidentally, do you know where *Clotted Cream's* logbook is?'

'I haven't seen it, so Tom probably left it on the yacht. Do you want it?'

Dexter nodded.

'I need to see what happened on the sea trials to get the full picture of what still has to be done. I can work out a rough estimate then of how much more money you're likely to need for running repairs and adjustments to equipment.'

'Come on, then. I'll take you over in the launch,' Lara offered, glad of an opportunity to escape from the office and get out on the river.

Latest News

Once on board the yacht, Dexter helped Lara open the hatch doorway and they both went down into the hull.

Built for speed rather than comfort, the main cabin was a mass of navigational aids and electrical equipment. A small galley and a couple of bunks made up the spartan living area and the rest was storage space.

The logbook was in the drawer of the chart table and, whilst Dexter began his study, Lara headed down below to check that all the water-tight compartments were still dry.

'Everything all right down there?' Dexter called out after a few moments. 'Tom certainly had a rough passage home, with winds gusting at Force 10 at times. There were a few problems with the self-steering, too. That'll need sorting before you or anybody else takes her out.'

Lara looked at him as she came back up into the main cabin. Was he coming round to the idea of her competing in the race?

'Everything seems nice and dry down there. I'll take the logbook ashore. Gramps is sure to want to read it. Are you ready to go?'

Dexter nodded.

Once on deck he stood in the cockpit, looking over the stern of *Clotted Cream* towards the river mouth.

'There's something about these boats that makes you yearn for the open sea, isn't there?' he said quietly.

'Do you do much sailing these days?' Lara asked.

'Not a lot.' Dexter shrugged. 'I had to sell my boat when I went to the States. I'm lucky that I've got friends who invite me to crew for them, but these days I'm rarely in the country.'

'We could go for a sail early tomorrow morning if you like,' Lara offered. 'That's my boat over there.' She pointed to *It's Mine!* on her mooring fifty yards up river.

'You're on,' Dexter said. 'Six o'clock too early for you?'

'No, that's fine.' Lara smiled. 'Come on. We'd better get back. I want you to go through those figures and tell me how much more money we need to keep *Clotted Cream* on course for the race.'

Mai was in the kitchen when they got back, filling Cassie in on the latest news about Tom.

'His right leg is broken in two places and his left in one. Thankfully, all the breaks are below the knee, but he'll still be in plaster for weeks.'

'What about his other injuries?' Cassie asked.

'The doctors are confident that his internal bruising is just that — bruising. He'll be in a wheelchair for some time, but the good news is he should be home by the end of next week.'

'So I can definitely see him tomorrow?' Lara asked eagerly.

'Yes. He's looking forward to your visit.' Mai smiled.

'We'll have to sort out where he's going to stay once he's discharged,' Cassie said thoughtfully. 'River View is obviously out of the question, with all those steps leading up to it and the spiral staircase inside.'

'Could we put a bed in your sitting-room?' Mai asked, indicating the small room that led off the kitchen. 'It's all on one level and Tom would be able to be a part of things.'

'He could direct operations from here, too,' Lara said.

Mai looked puzzled, but it was Cassie who answered.

'Lara wants to compete in the race instead of Tom. She says there's too much at stake simply to withdraw *Clotted Cream*. But nothing has been decided yet.' Cassie cast an anxious glance at her daughter.

'We need to have a family conference. Tom will have the final say.'

★ ★ ★

It was around six o'clock that evening when the telephone rang yet again. Cassie and Anna were in the kitchen, looking through the house details Anna had found.

'I can't face another sympathetic enquiry about Tom,' Cassie said. 'Would you answer it, please?' She carried on studying the estate agent's handouts.

'Seven o'clock? Fine. See you then.'

Anna put the phone down.

'That was James, phoning to remind you about the theatre. He's collecting you in an hour.'

Cassie sighed.

'I'd forgotten all about it. I'll ring back and cancel. I can't possibly go out tonight. I'm too tired.'

'Of course you can go. It'll take your mind off things.'

'What about supper? And there's Dexter. I can't just go out and leave him to his own devices.'

'I'll cook supper for everyone. And I'm sure between Lara, Mai and myself, we'll manage to entertain Dexter for a couple of hours.'

'But . . .'

'Not another word. Go and get ready,' Anna ordered.

Up in her bedroom, Cassie stood staring out of the window for a few moments. All she wanted to do was curl up in bed and sleep.

But Anna was probably right. It was ages since she'd been to the theatre. A good play might take her mind off things and help her feel better.

By the time she headed downstairs, James was already waiting, so they set off straight away.

'I thought a pre-theatre drink and then supper afterwards?' James said on the way into town. 'I've booked a table at the Stage Door. Is that OK with you?'

'The pre-theatre drink sounds nice, but I'm not too sure I'll be awake for supper afterwards. I didn't get much sleep last night.'

'How is Tom?'

By the time Cassie had filled him in on all the details, they were parking in town.

Whether it was the effect of the glass of wine James bought her or simply his pleasant company, Cassie began to relax. As they crossed the street to the theatre, James took her arm and, to her surprise, she found some comfort in his action.

The play, a well-known farce, certainly cheered Cassie up and she had to wipe tears of laughter from her face as the curtain came down on the last act. As well as banishing her exhaustion, the laughter seemed to have triggered her appetite and to James's delight she agreed to supper after all.

Much later, they drove back into the boatyard.

'Thank you for a lovely evening, James. I really enjoyed it. Would you like to come in for a coffee?' Cassie invited.

James shook his head.

'I'd love to, but I'd better get back. I enjoyed this evening, too. Perhaps we can have dinner one day next week? I'll give you a ring. And don't forget, if I can help in any way with regards to Tom, you just have to ask. Take care.'

'Shattered'

On Sunday morning, Cassie was up early enough to see Lara and Dexter sailing *It's Mine!* down river to the open sea. Lara was at the helm and Dexter was out on deck, tightening the main sail. Cassie smiled. Lara would be enjoying herself with Dexter on board to do some of the hard work.

She turned as Anna came into the kitchen.

'Morning. I was going to bring you breakfast in bed as a thank-you for everything you did yesterday,' Cassie said.

'Let's have it together instead.' Anna smiled. 'And you can finish looking at the house details and help me decide which ones to check out today.'

Out of the dozen or so leaflets Anna had collected, they narrowed it down to four.

'I really like the sound of this one,' Anna said. 'But it's right in the middle of town and I don't know whether I can cope with life as a townie. I've lived in the sticks for so long.'

'It would be a complete change. You'd certainly have everything on your doorstep.'

'I don't suppose there's any chance of you doing a recce with me today?'

Cassie shook her head.

'Sorry. Lara and I are visiting Tom later on, then we've got to have this family meeting.'

'Oh, well. Give Tom my love and tell him I'll be in to see him during the week.'

Tom was awake when Cassie and Lara walked into his small side ward later that day and was pleased to see them. But he looked tired and drawn and was still clearly in some pain, so they kept their visit short.

Cassie and Lara didn't talk much on the drive home. Cassie didn't want to be drawn into an argument, while Lara was preoccupied with Tom's reaction to the quick talk she'd had with him.

When Cassie had gone to have a word with the ward sister, Lara had taken the opportunity to ask Tom about the race.

Knowing that he wasn't really well enough to bother, she'd deliberately tried to keep her voice light.

'How would you feel about me skippering *Clotted Cream* in your place?'

'Shattered,' was his uncompromising reply. 'But I suppose I'll have to think about it.'

Mai had arrived then and Lara had had to be content with the thought that at least Tom hadn't instantly vetoed the idea.

Sitting beside her mother on the journey home, she tried to work out what would happen at the family conference that afternoon. She had a feeling that a lot would depend on Dexter.

Just then, her mobile phone rang.

It was Sebastian. Apparently he'd just heard about Tom's accident.

'Why didn't you let me know?' he complained to Lara. 'He is almost my brother-in-law.'

'I was going to e-mail you this evening with all the news,' Lara said.

'It sounds as if it'll be a while before

he's up and about again. Shame about the race. Give him my regards when you see him.'

'Of course. How are things with you?'

'OK. Should be in Gib tomorrow. After that, who knows? Very hush hush, this exercise. I'd better go. I'm on duty in fifteen minutes. Love you. E-mail me. 'Bye.'

Cassie looked at Lara. 'Sebastian' was all she'd mouthed by way of explanation at the beginning of the call.

'You haven't discussed your plan about the race with Sebastian, then?'

'Not yet. I'd rather wait until it's a *fait accompli*. He'll only try and talk me out of it.'

'I'm not the only one then,' Cassie said grimly.

Rufus, her brother, phoned shortly after she got home to say he and Bridget couldn't make the family get-together. They'd a meeting with a client who was talking about a permanent berth in the marina for his large motor-yacht.

'He's just the sort of customer we need to attract. Money no object,' Rufus said. 'So I don't want to cancel. As far as Lara and *Clotted Cream's* concerned I'm happy to let you and Dad decide.'

* * *

It was nearly four o'clock before everyone met up in Cassie's kitchen.

Dexter was the first to arrive.

'These are the figures I've worked out. Everything's quite easy to follow. I'm sure you'll reach the same conclusions as me when you go through them. Now, what time would you like me back?'

Cassie looked at him in surprise.

'But you're staying for the meeting, aren't you?'

Dexter shook his head.

'It's a family thing. I'd be intruding.'

'Nonsense. We need your expert input. Besides, I was hoping you'd be the calm, impartial voice of reason this afternoon,' Cassie said. 'Stop any family quarrels.' She smiled at him.

Dexter was silent for a few moments.

'OK. But I warn you, you mightn't like everything I have to say.'

'Deadline'

The figures, as Dexter went on to explain, indicated that, with Tom at the helm of *Clotted Cream*, there was enough money and sponsorship for a successful entry.

'Whether all the sponsors would remain committed if Lara were to take her brother's place is open to question,' he continued.

'If you withdraw, the deposit Tom paid as his initial registration fee is non-refundable. If you resubmit with Lara, or somebody else as replacement skipper, you'll need to pay the remaining seven and a half thousand pounds. The good news is that if the race committee reject the replacement application, you'll get that money back.' Dexter paused.

'Trouble could come if the race committee accept the new skipper but the sponsors don't and withdraw their support.'

'What are the chances of the race committee accepting Lara?' Liz Holdsworth asked.

'It's difficult to say. They'd probably prefer someone older and with more experience. Lara is only just old enough to enter. But, on the plus side, she's done lots of sailing and competed in a single-handed race already.'

There was a short silence and then Bill spoke up bluntly.

'Do you think she's up to it?'

Dexter hesitated, looking at Cassie and Lara before he answered.

'With certain reservations, yes,' he said finally.

Cassie sighed inwardly. Lara would be even more determined now.

'Has anybody spoken to Tom about all this?' Liz asked. '*Clotted Cream* is his boat.'

'I mentioned it this morning,' Lara

admitted. 'He promised he'd think about it.'

'I'm not sure there's time for that,' Dexter said. 'I really need to take the balance of the entrance fee and the replacement skipper details with me when I leave tomorrow — otherwise you'll miss the deadline.'

Bill took a deep breath.

'So we have to make a decision today, without Tom. Like Dexter. I have reservations, but I think Lara should be given the chance.'

'Gramps, thank you!' A delighted Lara leapt to her feet and hugged her grandfather. 'I won't let you or Tom down, I promise.'

'Still Angry?'

Dexter left early on Monday morning, taking Lara's application form and a cheque for the outstanding entry fee with him.

'When do you think we'll hear from

the race committee?' Cassie asked.

'Well, it's under five weeks to the race, so they'll have to respond quickly. You need all the time to fine tune things and to get the boat to Plymouth a fortnight before the start date. I think you should hear by the weekend.' He turned to Lara.

'You've got my mobile number. If you need any advice, give me a ring. If I can help, I will. Otherwise, I'll see you in Plymouth in three weeks. Good luck.'

He kissed Cassie on the cheek.

'Thanks for letting me stay. Tell Tom I'll see him soon. 'Bye.'

As they turned to go back into the house, Lara looked at her mother.

'Are you still angry with me?'

'I was never angry with you, just afraid. I've always known you'd want to follow in your dad's footsteps and be a sailor. I understand you see this as your chance to prove yourself, but I can't stop worrying about you — the same as I worry about Tom when he's away. And you must remember, I've already lost someone who meant the world to me.'

Lara didn't say anything. The unexpected bear hug in which she enveloped her mother was more expressive than any words.

The next few days passed in a blur for Cassie. There was so much to do. Normal office work for the boatyard had to take a back seat while she gave all her attention to organising the logistics of a round-the-world sail.

She was very grateful when Liz appeared in the office early on Tuesday morning and offered to take over the boatyard accounts again.

'Just until things get back to normal,' she said.

Cassie e-mailed all the sponsors, officially informing them of Tom's accident and telling them about Lara. She hoped they'd continue to offer her the same level of support as they had her brother.

There was good news from Daedalion Technological Sails. They'd finally agreed to supply *Clotted Cream* with the new sails she desperately needed. And they weren't worried about the change of skipper.

But then Liz took a phone call from Mr Hollis at the bank. He wanted Cassie to make an appointment to see him.

'She's very busy. Couldn't she telephone you?'

'I'd prefer to explain the position face to face,' Mr Hollis said.

Cassie groaned when her mother reported the conversation.

'It doesn't sound too good. I was positive the bank was going to sponsor us. We really do need their money.'

Bookings were also starting to arrive for the newly advertised sailing lessons and enquiring about accommodation on the barge. Cassie simply put those letters on one side. Mai would have to deal with them once Tom was home.

Anna put her house hunting on hold and took over the work on the barge. Mai helped her for a couple of hours every morning, but her days were mainly taken up with visiting Tom.

James rang, asking Cassie to have dinner with him on Friday evening.

'I'm sorry, but I can't this week. I'm so busy. Anna and I are working until eight or nine every evening and then we all just collapse with supper on a tray. And Friday evening I'd earmarked to convert the sitting-room into a bedroom, ready for Tom coming home.'

'How about I bring a take-away and a bottle of wine for you all? I'll come up by boat, so everything should stay warm. And then I'll give you a hand moving furniture.'

'What a lovely idea. Although I warn you, changing the sitting-room around is going to be hard work. Thanks, James. See you on Friday.'

Every day saw an improvement in Tom's general condition, but his spirits were low. He was finding it difficult to come to terms with the fact that it would be months before he was on his feet again.

For a few days, he couldn't even face Lara, which upset her greatly. Eventually, though, he rang her to apologise and promised to give her all the help he could.

'Not that I'll be much use, stuck in a wheelchair,' he added bitterly.

'Once you're home, I thought you could become my operations director,' Lara suggested tentatively. 'I really do need your expert knowledge. That way, too, you'd still be involved.'

'It's hardly the same, sis, you know that. But I'll do it for you. Just make sure you look after my boat.'

As promised, James arrived on Friday evening, bearing wine and fish and chips for everyone.

Supper was almost finished when the telephone rang.

'I'll get it,' Lara offered, jumping to her feet.

'Cassie, I need to talk to you,' James said quietly, choosing his moment.

'Why? What's wrong?'

'It's about the barge. Since Tom's

accident, the Harbour Commission have become concerned about your proposed sailing school.' He paused.

'They're going to refuse you a licence until the Health and Safety have inspected it and passed the barge as safe to have the public on board.'

'But it's already got a Health and Safety Certificate,' Cassie protested. 'Tom's accident was just that — a stupid accident because he was so tired. The barge itself is perfectly safe.'

'The fact that a handrail came away is what worries them. They want reassurance that everything is as it should be before they grant the licence. They've asked for another inspection.' He placed an envelope on the table.

'I've had to write you an official letter to that effect.' He looked at Cassie.

'I didn't want to post it. Please believe me, Cassie, when I say I tried to stop them taking this action. I know the barge is as safe as anything else on this river, but they refused to listen.'

'When will the Health and Safety visit?'

James shook his head.

'I don't know. They'll be writing to inform you.'

He glanced across the room as Lara put the telephone down and came back to them, her face serious.

'That was Dexter.'

Cassie waited. What now?

'He's just posted the letter informing me that my entry has been accepted by the race committee.' She let out a whoop of joy.

'I'm now the official skipper of *Clotted Cream*,' she added excitedly.

'Oh, well done, Lara,' James and Anna said together.

Cassie got up and put her arms around her.

'Yes. Congratulations, Lara.'

'What were you and James looking so serious about?'

'We have a problem with the barge.' Cassie filled Lara in on the latest developments.

'That's the official letter,' she said, indicating the unopened envelope on the table.

Cassie looked at everyone, suddenly feeling very tired.

'I just don't know how on earth I'm going to cope with Lara away at sea, Tom in a wheelchair and everything else going wrong.

'I wish to goodness we'd never bought that blasted barge. Tom wouldn't be in hospital and we wouldn't be in this mess.'

3

'A Good Story'

The day before Tom came home from hospital was also the moment the media woke up to the fact that Lara was to take his place in the round the world race.

The phone rang constantly and one or two reporters even turned up at the boatyard. With Lara out on the river, it was Cassie who had to deal with it all — on top of everything else.

When the telephone rang for the sixth time in as many minutes, she sighed as she picked it up. Thankfully, however, it was Dexter.

'Hi! How's Tom?'

'He's coming home tomorrow,' Cassie replied.

'That's great news.' Dexter sounded pleased. 'And how's the work progressing on *Clotted Cream?*' he went on.

'I think it's all going to plan,' Cassie said. 'But you'd really need to talk to Lara or Bill about that. My main problem at the moment is trying to deal with reporters.'

'From their point of view it's a good story,' Dexter pointed out. 'And your sponsors will be pleased with all the publicity.'

'Yes, of course. It's just the time it's taking up.' Cassie sounded exhausted. 'And there are still so many other things that have to be done.'

'I can probably help out with the Press, but I need to talk to Lara first. Is she around?' Dexter asked.

'She's working on *Clotted Cream*, but she's got her mobile with her.'

'Great! I'll give her a buzz right now. Talk to you later.'

Cassie had just begun to tackle the mountain of paperwork on her desk when Lara walked into the office.

'Don't talk to any more reporters, Mum.'

Cassie looked surprised.

'Why not?'

'Dexter has just suggested that I sell my story to one paper. Not only will it bring in some more money, it'll make things easier for you, too. He's got a contact in London. Hopefully they'll be in touch today.'

As if on cue, her mobile rang.

'Great. Thanks, Dexter, I know Mum will be pleased. Talk to you soon.'

Lara turned to Cassie.

'Sorted. Somebody will arrive tomorrow to interview me and take some photos, with Tom, too, if possible. They've also suggested I do a regular report from the boat — for another fee, of course.

'Oh, before I forget, Gramps wants to know if there's any news on when we can expect the self-steering gear back?'

'Not yet. Tell him not to be so impatient. It's only been gone five days and they did say it would take about eight. I'll start to chase tomorrow.

'By the way, have you told Sebastian

you're doing the race yet?' Cassie asked as Lara was about to head off.

'No. I was going to e-mail him last night but I was too tired.'

'If you don't tell him soon he'll read it in the newspaper and that won't go down very well,' Cassie pointed out.

'You're right, Mum. I'll do it this evening.'

As Lara closed the door behind her the phone rang again. This time it was Rule of Thumb Technology, confirming one of their technicians would be available to be part of the shore crew that would meet Lara in all the mandatory ports of call.

The first of these would be Cape Town, a mere thirty days after the start, if all went well. In the meantime the technician was on his way to Devon to help prepare the boat for the start.

Cassie felt relieved. The more experienced hands there were to ensure the safety of Lara and *Clotted Cream*, the happier she felt.

A Crucial Role

Later that morning Cassie made her way down to the barge to find Anna clearing up the mess made by the workmen repairing the companionway rail broken in Tom's accident.

'It's looking good,' Anna said. 'I'm sure the Health and Safety visit won't be a problem.'

She glanced at her friend, remembering how Cassie had reacted the night James had told her about the Harbour Commission calling in the Health and Safety, how tired and depressed she'd looked.

'I hope not,' Cassie said now. 'There were more enquiries in today's post about booking lessons and accommodation. Once Tom's home, he and Mai will be able to start organising that side of things at least.' She sighed.

'The trouble is, I keep feeling that we've taken on too much with the barge. Teaching people to sail is fine, but doing the catering for them as well means a lot more work.'

'Everything will settle down into a routine once Tom's home and all the race preparations are finished. You'll be able to concentrate on things here then,' Anna said. 'And I'll help whenever I can. Do you know what time Tom will be home tomorrow?' she asked.

'Around midday,' Cassie replied. 'At least the sitting-room is ready for him.'

James had been as good as his word, helping them to rearrange sofas and beds. He'd even dragged a large desk in from the storeroom to take all the equipment Tom would need if he were to take on the role of Lara's Operations Director.

Cassie had already put some of the files on the table, along with a fax machine, copier, telephone and all the wires and modems ready for the brand-new computer the technician from Rule of Thumb would be bringing.

She wanted Tom to know that his

new role of Operations Director was crucial, that he was still important to the success of *Clotted Cream* even if he wasn't at the tiller. Lara needed his experienced input.

Confrontation

It was unfortunate that Tom arrived within minutes of the reporter the next morning and what should have been a happy homecoming turned into a confrontation.

Nobody had remembered to tell Tom about the deal Lara had made with the newspaper and he objected to being photographed by what he thought was an opportunist cameraman.

Sharply telling the photographer to 'Put that camera away,' he totally refused even to think about having his picture taken.

In the end Cassie suggested Lara take the reporter out to *Clotted Cream*.

'They'll want some photographs of

you on the boat so you might as well do the interview out there. When you get back, hopefully Tom will have found his manners again,' Cassie said grimly.

Tom had the decency to look ashamed and muttered something that Cassie took to be an apology.

'Right,' she said, 'let's get you indoors and settled.'

Between them, Cassie and Mai re-arranged pillows, made Tom some lunch and generally tried to make him comfortable.

'The reporter will want to talk to you as well as Lara — and take your photograph with her. That was part of the deal,' Mai said eventually. 'Do you feel up to it this afternoon? Or shall I ask him to come back tomorrow?'

Tom sighed.

'Quite honestly, I feel exhausted. If I could have a bit of a sleep before I see him, that would help. I promise to be good.' He glanced at Cassie as he said this.

'I'm sorry I was rude earlier. I know

it's no excuse, but I'm finding it hard to accept I'm going to be out of action for so long. And Lara taking my place just seems to be rubbing it in.'

'I'm sorry you feel like that,' Cassie said. 'But it's the way it is. And, remember, it's stopping *Clotted Cream* from being a drain on the boatyard finances whilst you're laid up.'

*   *   *

Tom was still asleep when Lara brought the reporter back to the house, so it was mid-afternoon before he got the photograph he wanted of Tom and Lara together.

Tom chatted politely for a few minutes, but it soon became clear that he was still exhausted and needed to rest.

Once the reporter had left, and Lara had gone back to finish some work on the boat, Anna insisted that Cassie went for a walk with her.

'Mai's here to look after Tom. Some

exercise and fresh air will perk you up.'

They set out companionably along the riverbank path.

'Have you made an appointment to see any houses yet?' Cassie asked.

'I've viewed a couple of totally unsuitable ones, but I've two more promising places lined up for next week. One's in Castle Gardens and the other's the one in town I showed you the details of.' Anna paused before continuing.

'James has asked me to stay in town and have dinner with him afterwards.' She glanced apprehensively at Cassie as if unsure of her reaction to this news.

'That's nice for you. He's good company and you'll enjoy the Riverside Café,' Cassie said, assuming that James would take Anna to his favourite local restaurant. 'The food's really good there.'

'You don't mind?' Anna asked.

'No. Why on earth should I?' Cassie said. 'James is a free agent. Come on, let's make for that willow and then turn back. I'm glad you talked me into this walk. I'm really enjoying it.'

Increasing her pace to keep up with her friend, Anna didn't have the breath to enlighten her that James had suggested the Seafarers Restaurant at the Country Club for dinner — a far more expensive and exotic location than the Riverside Café.

Furious

Early that evening, Lara sat in her room, staring at her computer screen. She was trying to compose an e-mail to Sebastian and it wasn't going well.

Dear Sebastian, she typed. That was the easy bit. She knew he was going to be furious about her taking Tom's place in the race, no matter how she broke the news.

She glanced across at the red velvet ring box on her dressing-table. Sebastian had been upset when she hadn't immediately accepted his proposal.

She'd promised him she'd think about it whilst he was away.

He'd insisted on giving her his ring.

'Next time we see each other, I hope you'll be wearing it,' he'd said, sounding confident that this indeed would be the case.

It was a beautiful ring — a large ruby surrounded by diamonds — the sort of ring anybody would be proud to wear. As yet, though, she hadn't even tried it on.

Lara sighed. What on earth was her problem? She loved Sebastian. So why was she so afraid of committing herself to marrying him?

She took a deep breath and started to type again.

I hope the exercise is going well. Tom's home, but he's finding it difficult to cope with the thought of being out of action for so long.

Sebastian didn't like receiving long e-mails. He said the whole point of e-mails was that they were short and to the point. Perhaps she should come straight out with it.

Also, he's a bit jealous I've got the go ahead to race Clotted Cream *in his place. But he has agreed to be my Operations Director. I'm so sorry for Tom, but pleased I've got the chance to prove myself.*

The bad news is that it means I'll still be at sea when you get back. It'll be nearly six months before we see each other again. I'll miss you so much, but at least we can still e-mail whilst I'm away. Love you, Lara.

She hesitated a fraction of a second before hitting the 'send' button and watched as the message disappeared from the screen. It was done. At least there wouldn't be a face-to-face confrontation.

The e-mail she sent to Dexter was much easier to compose. In fact, it turned out to be quite lengthy, telling him all about *Clotted Cream's* progress and how she hoped to be doing her sea trials soon.

Hopefully he liked receiving long

rambling e-mails as opposed to short pithy ones.

Finally Lara shut down her computer and walked across to the dressing-table. Picking up the ring box, she opened a drawer and buried it in amongst her jumpers.

She'd forget about it until after the race. She had too much to do right now to make such an important decision. Maybe by the time she came back, her feelings would be a whole lot clearer.

Back To Normal

Heading downstairs, she found Cassie, Mai and Anna in the sitting-room, talking to Tom. A few hours' sleep seemed to have done him the world of good and he sounded a lot more cheerful.

'Hi, sis,' he greeted her. 'You're just in time to join us for a glass of wine.'

'I thought we were going to check through the medical supplies tonight?'

Lara said, glancing at Cassie.

'There's still time. We're just celebrating Tom's first night home,' Cassie said.

Taking her glass, Lara perched on the edge of Tom's bed and clinked her glass with his.

'Welcome home. You know, you didn't have to break both legs,' she said cheekily, 'one would have done. But thanks anyway.'

'Here's to you, Lara,' Tom said. 'But be warned, little sister, if you don't bring *Clotted Cream* back home in one piece, I'll break *your* legs!'

Cassie listened to the pair of them sparring, relieved that things seemed to be back to normal between them.

The next few weeks would be as tough on Tom as they would be on Lara. He'd have his own battles to fight, both physically as his legs mended, and mentally as he helped Lara achieve what he longed to be doing himself.

'As enjoyable as this is,' Lara announced, finishing her glass and standing up, 'some of us still have work to do. I'm off to the office. I'll see you tomorrow, brother dear.' She kissed Tom lightly on the cheek.

Cassie joined her five minutes later, just as Lara was lifting a large cardboard box filled with medical supplies on to the table.

'No sign of the freeze-dried food-stuffs?' Lara asked.

Cassie shook her head.

'Not yet. They've promised delivery within the next few days.'

Lara put some sealed syringes on the table.

'If you call out the items I'll tick them off the check list,' Cassie said. 'There's an awful lot here. Heaven forbid you ever have to use any of it.'

She looked at the DIY kit for setting broken bones and the ready-threaded needles for sewing up deep cuts and shivered apprehensively.

'These days it's a case of being prepared for any eventuality. Like rescuing somebody who's injured,' Lara added quickly.

'The painkillers might get taken if I have one of my migraines, but otherwise this lot will hopefully all come back unused.'

'I remember the medical box your dad took on his trips,' Cassie said slowly.

'It had a large packet of plasters, an antiseptic spray, a pair of scissors, bandages and a small tub of painkillers. How times have changed. Oh, and Dad always put a small bottle of brandy in. Purely medicinal, he always said.' She smiled at Lara.

'The brandy was always gone when he got home. Funny, that.'

Lara laughed as she put her hand into the box and pulled out a bottle of brandy.

'I didn't realise it was a family tradition.'

There was a short silence while Cassie looked at Lara.

'You will take . . . '

Lara interrupted her before she could finish the sentence.

'Mum, I know what you're going to say and it's as pointless as me telling you not to worry. I know nothing will stop you worrying about me until the race is over and I'm home again.

'And you know deep down that, yes, I will take care, but you also know that I will take risks if I have to.'

'You wouldn't be Dad's girl if you didn't,' Cassie said shakily.

Sea Trials

Over the next few days, things settled down into something of a routine.

Now that Tom was home, Mai was able to divide her time between looking after him and working on the barge. With Liz in charge of the routine office work and Anna helping out wherever needed, Cassie and Lara threw themselves into the preparations for the race.

Within a few days of being home Tom had taken up his role as Operations Director and by ten o'clock most mornings he was in his wheelchair in front of the computer.

A day after the self-steering was refitted, Lara took off on her much-needed sea trials. The plan was for her to go down the Channel, get clear of the shipping lanes and spend some time sailing the Atlantic, before turning and heading for home.

Standing in the cockpit, Lara kept a firm hand on *Clotted Cream's* tiller, concentrating hard on maintaining a steady course and trying to keep her excitement under control.

Once out in the river mouth she moved forward to hoist the jib sail and felt a tremor of exhilaration flood her body as the yacht responded to the pull of the small sail by leaping forward into the waves.

Already the spray on her face and the feel of the boat moving beneath her feet was filling her with happy anticipation.

Ahead of her lay the Channel with its busy shipping lanes and then the relatively open space of the North

Atlantic Ocean, space in which she would begin to get to know *Clotted Cream's* idiosyncrasies before they started on her dream voyage together. It was a voyage on which she was determined to show everybody just what she was capable of.

Cassie and Bill followed in the launch as *Clotted Cream* made her way out of the river and into the Channel. As Lara cut the engine and hoisted the main sail, she turned and waved goodbye.

'See you in three days,' she shouted as the yacht began to speed through the water. Minutes later she was a mere speck in the distance.

Bill turned the launch and slowly they made their way into the river mouth, heading towards the harbour.

Bill had to collect some spare parts from the garage and Mai had asked Cassie to pick up a prescription for Tom, so Bill took the launch alongside the public quay.

'See you back here in what? Ten minutes?' Bill said as they went off in opposite directions.

Errands completed, Cassie popped into the newsagent's on her way back to the launch. She wanted a copy of the local paper.

Standing by the till waiting to pay, she glanced at the front page and felt her body stiffen.

Under the headline *Local Girl Keeps Family Name To The Foresail* was a colour picture of a smiling Lara on board *Clotted Cream*. Halfway down the page was another picture — an old black and white one of a beaming Miles. Cassie recognised it instantly as having been taken after his Round Britain win. His last race.

Bill was deep in conversation with James when Cassie arrived back at the quay.

'Anything interesting in that local rag, then?' Bill asked.

'Oh, yes.' Cassie nodded, holding the front page up for them both to see.

'It's a good picture of Lara,' Bill said. 'What do they say about her?'

'I haven't read it yet,' Cassie answered. 'The other picture rather took me aback. I wasn't expecting it.'

'I read the article earlier,' James said. 'Apart from the terrible headline, it's a good report, wishing her *bon voyage* and all that. The picture of Miles was just to make the family tradition link — how she's following in Dad's footsteps.'

'That's the last thing anybody wants to happen in this race!' Cassie snapped at him, bursting into tears.

'Can we go, please, Dad?' she begged as she scrambled into the launch.

Bill started the engine as a stricken James untied the ropes and cast them off.

'Cassie, I'm so sorry,' he said. 'I didn't think before I spoke. I wouldn't upset you for the world, you know that.'

Cassie shook her head and tried to smile.

'I know, James. It's just that it's always at the back of my mind.'

There was no time for anyone to say

any more as the launch moved further away from the quay. James stood watching for several moments before sighing and heading back to his office.

They chugged their way upriver with Bill at the tiller.

'He's a nice man, James,' Bill said casually after a few minutes.

Cassie sniffed, her tears starting to dry up.

'Yes, I know. I'll ring him later to apologise for shouting at him.'

Bill looked intently at Cassie.

'You know, love, you've got to start living again. Tom's happily married. Lara's doing her own thing. They're not children any longer. You can't go on living your life through them and constantly worrying about whether they're going to suffer the same fate as Miles.'

'Is that what you and Mum think I've done all these years?' Cassie asked, feeling the tears pricking the back of her eyes again.

'We knew you'd take a long time

getting over losing Miles,' Bill told his daughter quietly. 'But when he died it was as if you stopped living, too. I know how much you loved him, Cassie, but twenty years is a long time to grieve.'

He steered the launch around some flotsam before speaking again.

'Your mum and I kept hoping that you'd meet someone new, someone who'd love you and bring you back to the real world. I'm sorry it hasn't happened, but I don't want to see you wasting any more of your life.

'Tom and Lara are a credit to you. Stop worrying about them and concentrate on getting your own life sorted.'

Jealousy?

When Cassie and Bill got back to the boatyard they noticed Mai saying goodbye to a small blonde woman. Father and daughter exchanged a glance. Her businesslike dark suit wasn't exactly the normal gear for climbing around on boats.

Mai spotted them and she and Cassie walked back to the house together.

'That was Mrs Catchpole, Health and Safety Inspector,' Mai said.

Cassie glanced at her quickly.

'And?'

'I think everything's going to be OK. She looked at all the handrails, not just the one broken in Tom's accident. She wants them all adapted to the same standard as the replacement, and some more safety catches on the two forward hatches. Basically, that's it.

'She's going to put everything in writing, but she doesn't see a problem with issuing a licence in time for the season.'

'Thank goodness for that.'

'Oh, I nearly forgot,' Mai said. 'The supplies you and Lara were waiting for arrived today. They're in the office. All twelve boxes.'

Cassie groaned.

'Didn't Anna ask the driver to take them straight down to the yard ready for loading on *Clotted Cream* when Lara gets back?'

Mai shook her head.

'Anna isn't here. She's gone to look at houses, remember? And then she's having dinner with James.'

Cassie had forgotten about Anna's date with James. To her surprise, her heart constricted at the thought of the two of them together and she felt a pang of . . . jealousy?

But that was ridiculous. As she'd said to Anna, she and James were just friends. He was free to see anyone he chose.

Nevertheless, in light of the conversation she'd just had with her father, it suddenly dawned on Cassie that she was letting her life — and her chances of happiness — slip by.

All thoughts of James were banished to the back of her mind, however, as soon as she and Mai walked into the house.

'Hi!' Tom greeted them cheerfully. 'How did the Health and Safety go?'

he asked Mai. 'Will we get our certificate?'

Mai nodded.

'Cassie can tell you all about it while I get some supper organised. You need to talk about the other problem we have with the barge, too.' Mai disappeared into the kitchen.

'What other problem?' Cassie asked bluntly.

'We've been going through the paperwork and checking how the bookings are coming in,' Tom said. He pulled a file towards him.

'The response to the brochures has been good, I thought,' Cassie said. 'You and Mai should have a flourishing business there in a couple of seasons.'

'In theory, you're right, Mum, but — ' Tom paused. 'Our first booking is for a party of five teenagers in a month's time. They all want cabins on the barge, which isn't a problem, and they all want sailing lessons, which is.'

Cassie looked at him, puzzled.

'Why? The barge was bought as a

base for your sailing school.' Her voice trailed away as she suddenly realised the problem.

'I won't be able to teach until this season is virtually over. Mai isn't qualified. Besides, she has the catering side to deal with. Lara won't be here. The problem is we don't have a sailing instructor.'

There was a short silence before Cassie spoke.

'We'll just have to hire someone for a few weeks until you're back on your feet again.'

'There's not enough money in the kitty to do that for very long,' Tom pointed out. 'The renovation and fitting out has taken more than we expected and now there's the extra work the Health and Safety want for the new licence.

'There is another solution,' Tom said slowly.

'You taught Lara and me to sail. You could do it until I'm out of this thing.' He thumped the arms of his wheel-chair.

'That was different,' Cassie protested. 'I haven't sailed a dinghy for years.'

'You still have an RYA teaching qualification.'

He was looking directly at her, and Cassie had to take a deep breath. This was the very last thing she wanted to do . . .

4

Time To Think

Cassie went up to her room after supper, Tom's words ringing in her ears.

'You can do it, Mum. You know you can.'

But she had no intention of teaching sailing — even for a couple of weeks. They'd just have to sort something else out.

Upstairs, Cassie switched on the radio and lay down on the bed, hands behind her head. She needed some time on her own, to think about what her father had said in the launch on the way home.

It was true. Twenty years of her life had gone by — not without her noticing, but certainly without her playing a leading part in it.

To the outside world she assumed

she'd appeared whole. She was Tom and Lara's mum, indistinguishable from their friends' mothers, getting on with her life. But inwardly she'd never emerged from the lethargy she'd allowed to creep over her the day Miles was reported missing.

At first, it had been easier to live in the past with her memories and exist through the children, rather than get out and create a new life for herself. After a few years it had become an ingrained habit she seemed incapable of changing.

She reached over and picked up the silver-framed photograph from her bedside table and studied the young couple who smiled out at her.

The colours of this last photograph of herself and Miles were fading. Like her, the image was beginning to show its age.

Miles, though, had never grown old.

Just then, there was a knock on the door. Cassie hastily put the picture back in its place and stood up.

'Yes?'

'It's Anna. May I come in?'

'Of course.'

'Are you all right?' Anna asked. 'It's not like you to hide away in your room.'

'I needed some time to think. I've issues to sort out. It was something Dad said, actually. He reckons it's about time I started to get a life of my own.'

'New Start'

Cassie sat back down on the bed and looked at her friend.

'Do you think the same?'

Anna nodded.

'I think you've missed out on a lot of things you could have done — would have done, if things had been different. I've only been a widow for five years, but I know how hard it is to come to terms with it.'

'Do you still miss Harry?'

Anna smiled ruefully.

'Yes, of course. It's no easier being on your own after twenty-five years of marriage than it is after seven. But life goes on and I think moving away from the farm will be good for me.

'Have you ever thought about moving away?'

Cassie shook her head.

'No. Where on earth would I go? All my family and friends are here.' She sighed.

'I'll have to try to make my new start on home ground.'

'I hope you mean it, Cassie. You've hidden away from the world for far too long.'

Cassie stood up and straightened the bedspread.

'So, how was your day?' she asked Anna. 'Did you like either of the houses? And how did your meal with James go?'

'The one in Castle Gardens is nice, but too small. As for the house in town, I'm really tempted. Will you come and see it with me and give me your honest opinion?'

'Of course. How about tomorrow?'

'Great. We'll take my car and I'll treat us to lunch,' Anna said.

'So how was the Riverside tonight? Did you enjoy you meal?' Cassie asked again.

'James took me to the Seafarers.'

'Gosh, that was pushing the boat out a bit!' Cassie looked surprised.

'I got the feeling I wasn't the one he really wanted to treat. He spent most of the evening talking about you, about how nice you are and how he regrets upsetting you.'

'I meant to phone him and apologise for my outburst,' Cassie said. 'It wasn't his fault at all. It was me over-reacting.'

'Well, he should be home by now. Why don't you phone him? I'm sure he'd be only too pleased to be a part of your new start.' Anna laughed as she said it but her eyes were serious as she looked at Cassie.

James was home when she phoned a few minutes later and was pleased to hear from her, as Anna had predicted.

'I'm sorry I was so rude, James.' Cassie got straight to the point. 'I don't normally snap at people. Please forgive me.'

'Consider it done. I realise you're under a lot of strain right now.' There was a short pause before he went on. 'Would you like to have dinner with me on Saturday evening?'

'That would be nice, thank you. There's something I'd like to ask you then as well.'

'Ask me now.'

'No. It'll keep. I'll see you on Saturday.'

As Cassie replaced the receiver she wondered whether her question for James would in fact keep, or whether she'd have changed her mind by Saturday and lost her nerve.

Wealthy Client

It was raining hard the next morning as Cassie and Anna prepared to leave for town. Cassie nearly suggested putting their outing off but Anna was so keen to show her the house that she didn't have the heart even to suggest it.

Lara sent an e-mail just before they left which they read over Tom's shoulder.

My first night on Clotted Cream was wonderful. The self-steering is working a dream. Weather good so far, but there's a depression forecast. Hopefully I'll be able to skirt around the edge of it.

Turning for home about midday. See you all some time tomorrow morning. Love, Lara.

P.S. Any chance of a curry for dinner tomorrow, Mum?

'If you're e-mailing or speaking to her, Tom, tell her yes,' Cassie said, adding the ingredients to her shopping list.

'Right, we're off to brave the rain. We'll hand in these barge brochures for Rufus on our way. See you later.'

Cassie and Anna ran into the marina

reception office, both clutching a box of brochures. Rufus was talking to a tall man dressed in expensive wet weather gear.

'Cassie, Anna, meet Doug Hampshire. He's berthing his yacht down on Pontoon E for the next year.'

As Pontoon E was reserved for the largest, most expensive boats, Cassie reckoned Doug must be the wealthy client Rufus had been so keen to sign up.

She smiled at Doug as he took her hand in a firm grip.

'Pleased to meet you,' he said. 'I'm having an 'Open Boat' for a couple of hours on Sunday, as an opportunity to meet some locals. I hope you'll both come? About six-thirty. You'll pass the word around, Rufus?'

Thanking Doug, Cassie and Anna made a dash for the car.

'Nice man,' Anna said. 'I wonder what his wife's like?'

Cassie shrugged, but there was a warmth in his eyes that made her think she must be a lucky woman.

Once in town, Anna collected the key from the estate agent and took Cassie to see Glebe House.

Situated down a lane off one of the main streets, Cassie saw immediately why it appealed to Anna.

Built at the turn of the nineteenth century, it stood squarely in what had clearly once been an orchard, and through the rain Cassie could see several gnarled apple trees dotted around the large garden.

A high redbrick wall around the entire perimeter of the property encased it in perfect solitude from its neighbours, creating a little bit of countryside in the heart of town.

Once they were inside, Cassie turned to Anna.

'I can see you living here. It's got such a wonderful feel about it — even on a day like today.'

The next hour flew by as they wandered from room to room, discussing the best way to redesign and decorate the house.

They finished the tour of inspection in the kitchen.

'The only thing I must have in here apart from the Aga is a dresser,' Anna declared.

'The only thing I must have right now is lunch!' Cassie said. 'I'm starving.'

'Come on, then. Let's take the key back. Shall I make an offer, do you think?' Anna asked seriously.

'You'd be mad not to,' Cassie said.

Anna, as promised, treated them to lunch in the old coaching inn on the embankment. Before leaving town they did some shopping and then headed slowly home.

As they drove into the yard Cassie was surprised to see Dexter's sports car parked in front of the house.

'Lovely to see you, Dexter,' she said. 'Tom didn't say you were coming. Are you staying?'

'It was a spur of the moment thing. And yes, please, if you can put up with me. I'm on my way down to Plymouth but I don't have to be there for a couple of days.'

Supper that evening was a jolly affair. Tom was pleased to see his old friend and as they all gathered around the table, he and Dexter were soon deep in reminiscences about the times they'd sailed together and the races they'd won.

Because Tom was hemmed in and unable to move quickly, it was Dexter who got up to answer the satellite phone when Lara called.

'No problems to report? Good. So we'll see you tomorrow about midday? Do you want to talk to Cassie? Tom? OK, I'll give everyone your love. Take care out there,' he said.

'Everything is fine.' He turned to Cassie. 'She's planning on having something to eat then getting some sleep so she'll be awake and ready to tackle the busiest part of the Channel tomorrow. She sends her love to everyone.'

'Are You Engaged?'

The next morning Cassie and Dexter were down on the landing pontoon as Lara motored up river. They both gave her a hand securing *Clotted Cream* alongside.

Within minutes the shore crew from Rule of Thumb Technology were on board checking out all the electronics, and plans were made to begin loading provisions that afternoon.

'Did you have much trouble trimming the boat?' Dexter asked, looking at Lara's slight frame and remembering how difficult it had been for him to balance the last boat he'd raced properly.

Lara shook her head.

'Not really. The only problem is, with the wind continually changing direction, you know that you'll be shifting it all back again within a few hours. Hopefully, during the race itself, the wind will be more consistent.'

'Probably be much stronger, too,' was

Dexter's only comment as he picked up Lara's sail-bag ready to go ashore.

That afternoon, Lara and Dexter loaded and packed provisions into *Clotted Cream*'s hold with an easy familiarity. As they walked back to the house, Lara turned to Dexter.

'Thanks a lot for your help. I really appreciate it.'

Dexter glanced at her before replying.

'I gather from Tom that your boyfriend is worried about you doing this trip?'

Lara shrugged.

'Mum's worried, too. But she hasn't said I shouldn't.'

'And he has?'

Lara just pulled a face and didn't answer.

'Are you and he engaged?' he persisted.

'No.' Lara shook her head. She didn't feel the need to tell Dexter about the ring box hidden in her drawer — or about the doubts she was having about her feelings for Sebastian.

She had enough to think about right now.

The next twenty-four hours were busy ones. Everybody in the boatyard and marina was roped in to help with all the preparations necessary to get Lara and *Clotted Cream* ready for their big adventure.

As Cassie told James over dinner at the Seafarers on Saturday evening, she found it hard to believe how quickly the race date was approaching — and how much work was involved.

'Honestly, James, there are far more regulations these days compared with twenty years ago. And the amount of paperwork is unbelievable!'

'A lot more people are involved, I suppose,' James said. 'Like everything else, it's big business these days, too.' He glanced at her.

'How did Lara cope with her sea trials? *Clotted Cream's* a big boat to manage single-handed.'

'Fine. Lara is very determined. She

feels if Ellen MacArthur can race Open 60s, so can she!'

They were eating dessert when James turned the conversation.

'Well, Cassie, what was the question you wanted to ask me?'

Cassie put her spoon down and took a deep breath.

'You once asked me to go sailing with you.'

James nodded.

'Yes, I remember. The invitation still stands.'

'In that case, will you please take me out as soon as possible?'

There, the words were spoken.

'Of course. Monday afternoon OK?'

'Thank you.' Cassie smiled.

'May I ask what brought about the change of mind?'

Cassie was reluctant to tell him the truth — that she had some ghosts to lay. She didn't want him to think she was using him.

'Oh, I just wanted to find out if I still remembered how to do it after all this time,' she said instead.

To her ears the reason seemed shallow, but James appeared to accept it.

'I don't think you ever forget,' he said simply, placing his hand over hers in a comforting gesture that felt to Cassie suddenly too intimate.

To her relief, an attentive waiter appeared with the offer of coffee and she was able to reclaim her hand without undue fuss. As much as she liked James, she wasn't ready for any complications in their relationship.

'My social life suddenly seems to be taking off,' she said brightly. 'I haven't been so busy in years. Here I am tonight with you, we're going sailing next week and tomorrow it's the 'open boat' party. Are you going?'

'Yes. It's not really my sort of thing, but I have to put in an appearance. Doug Hampshire seems nice enough.'

'Rufus says his boat is amazing — the last word in luxury. He reckons it should be moored in St Tropez rather than here!'

'A Floating Palace'

Cassie was inclined to agree with her brother the next evening, as she, Lara and Anna climbed aboard *Megabyte*.

'Now we know how he made his money,' Lara observed. 'Computers.'

'Wow!' Anna exclaimed. 'It's a floating palace. Perhaps you ought to talk to him about some sponsorship for *Clotted Cream*.'

'Come on,' Cassie said to Lara, 'I'll introduce you.' The three women moved across the thick cream carpet of the main saloon towards Doug, who was standing by an ornate dining-table laden with food and drink, talking to Mai, Dexter and James.

'No sign of Mrs Hampshire, is there?' Anna whispered.

Cassie, looking round at the opulent furnishings, the original paintings on the walls, the priceless ornaments placed strategically, had to keep telling herself that she was on board a boat. It felt more like a very expensive and exclusive hotel.

But Anna was right. With nothing personal or feminine on display, one couldn't help wondering about the existence of a Mrs Hampshire.

'All ready for your big adventure, Lara?' Doug asked, after the introductions had been made.

She nodded.

'I can't wait. There's the trip to Plymouth tomorrow, ten days' final sorting out and then it's all go.'

'Are you going to Plymouth, too?' Doug asked Cassie.

'I'm planning on being there for the start of the race,' Cassie said. 'I'd hate to miss that. Otherwise, work here calls.'

'I've organised a berth down there for *Megabyte* for the weekend of the race start. I hope you'll all join me on board. Then we can go out to sea and give Lara a proper send-off.'

In Style

Cassie smiled her thanks at Doug. She had been wondering how she was going to manage to join the flotilla of boats that always followed competitors out to the line at the start of a big race. Going on Doug's boat, she'd certainly be seeing Lara off in style.

'My daughter Vanessa — ' he inclined his head in the direction of a tall, dark-haired girl talking to Mai ' — will be there. She's the one you need to talk to, Lara, if you want some additional sponsorship.'

'We could always do with extra money,' Lara said quickly. 'And the bank didn't come back to us about their offer after Tom's accident. If you'll excuse me, I'll go and have a word.'

Doug turned to Cassie.

'You'll have to excuse me, too. I think I'd better circulate. I'll see you later. Help yourself to food.' He waved his hand in the direction of the buffet.

'Not for me, thanks,' James said. 'I

have to be off. I'll see you tomorrow, Cassie. Two o'clock, down on your landing stage, OK?'

'I'll be there,' Cassie promised.

Both Anna and Mai looked at her as the two men left them, waiting for an explanation.

Cassie sighed.

'I'm going sailing with James tomorrow. And I'd appreciate it, Mai, if you don't mention it to Tom. I don't want him jumping to the wrong conclusion.'

Exhilarating

Despite getting up at five o'clock the next morning, Cassie still missed saying goodbye to Dexter. According to the note he left, he'd crept out of the house at 4.30 and hoped he hadn't disturbed anybody.

Thanks for having me. Tell Lara to have a good trip and I'll see her in Plymouth later. Dexter.

Drinking her coffee, Cassie thought

about the day ahead. Lara was planning to leave at noon for her trip to Plymouth.

Cassie realised Tom was still having a hard time accepting that Lara was taking his place, but he was hiding his feelings well. He'd given his sister all the support and advice he could. And Cassie knew that mentally he'd be with her on every wave of the voyage.

He even managed to make it to the pontoon to see her off. Lara came across to kiss him goodbye as the shore crew began to untie the moorings.

'Thanks, bruv. I'll see you. 'Bye,' she said gruffly.

'I'm coming to see you off next week, so no goodbyes,' Tom said. 'I want to make sure you've got *Clotted Cream* set up properly before we let you loose in the Atlantic.'

'But . . . ' Lara began, looking at Tom and then the wheelchair.

'But nothing. I'll be there,' Tom said, an edge to his voice.

As *Clotted Cream* motored down

river, Tom sat watching until she was too far away to focus on. Mai came over to move him.

'I'm fine,' he said quietly. 'Leave me for a bit.'

It was another half hour before he asked Mai to push him back to the house.

Cassie was back down on the landing stage in good time for her two o'clock meeting with James and nervously watched as he began to bring his small sailing yacht alongside to pick her up. Was she ready for this?

'I thought we'd go up to Salmon Creek. There's usually a bit of breeze up there. Do you want to steer while I get the sails?'

Cassie took the tiller from him and concentrated on steering the boat out through the mooring trots to the main channel. She was used to this, doing it several times during the course of a working week with the yard's launch.

Salmon Creek, though, was different. She rarely ventured that far up river.

There were too many memories associated with it. She and Miles had often gone there for an afternoon's sailing. Now, she was going with James.

She watched as he pulled up the mainsail and turned the outboard motor off as he hauled the jib sail up.

When he joined her in the cockpit she released the tiller and moved forward on deck, ready to do her bit with the sails when James changed course to take advantage of the fluctuating wind.

Without the noise of the outboard she could hear the natural sounds of the river — seagulls screeching, curlews on the mud banks calling their plaintive cries, the wind rustling through the trees. Even the noise of sheep bleating in distant fields drifted down on the wind.

As James called 'Jibe', Cassie automatically ducked, and the boom swung across, taking the mainsail to catch the wind now blowing from the east. And that was the start of an exhilarating hour during which James really put her through her paces and Cassie rediscovered her love of sailing.

'Thank you so much, James,' she said as they motored back down river. 'I really enjoyed that.'

'I told you, you never forget the basics. We must do it again. Fancy crewing for me in this year's regattas?'

'We'll see,' was all Cassie said.

Ghosts might have been laid, but it was too soon to commit herself to doing more of something that had once taken over her life.

★   ★   ★

Lara and the crew made good time getting to Plymouth. As they motored *Clotted Cream* into harbour and slowly eased their way into a berth between other competitors, Lara could almost taste the excitement in the air.

Dexter was on the quay to welcome her. He was part of the official race-organising committee and as soon as the yacht was secure he jumped on board.

'I'll give you five minutes to phone Cassie and tell her you've arrived safely,' he said, 'and then I have a mountain of paperwork to go through with you.'

Lara made them both a cup of coffee and they settled down to making sure everything was in order for *Clotted Cream* to take part in the race. As Dexter stamped the last official piece of paper, he looked at Lara.

'Before I take you to meet people, I have to say something.' He paused before continuing.

'You know you have only to ask for my help and I'll give it, but there may be times when it would be best for us not to appear too friendly. The other competitors . . . ' Dexter hesitated again.

'Might read the wrong thing into one of the organisers being too friendly with a competitor,' Lara finished for him.

'I know the score, Dexter. Don't worry.'

'Thanks for understanding, Lara. I didn't want you to feel that I was suddenly keeping my distance.'

He gave her a helping hand as she jumped on to the quay.

'Right,' he said, 'let's go and introduce you to some of the other competitors.'

Hero

Just as they turned to walk along the quay, Dexter's mobile phone rang.

'Sorry. Duty calls. I'm needed back in the office.' And he was gone.

Lara stood undecided for a second or two before starting to climb back on *Clotted Cream*. She'd meet everyone later.

'Hi, you must be Tom's little sister.'

She turned to see a huge bear-like man standing on the deck of the next yacht. Lara recognised him immediately as the world-famous solo yachtsman she regarded as one of the heroes of the sport.

'Want to join us for coffee?' he asked, indicating the group behind him.

Ten minutes later, sitting in the cockpit of the yacht, holding a mug of coffee, Lara wanted to pinch herself.

These fellow competitors of hers were all well-known sailors and they were taking her presence amongst them seriously.

They all knew Tom and were pleased to hear that he hoped to be in Plymouth for the start of the race.

It was as she moved to make room for yet another sailor to join them for coffee that she glanced across the quay and felt the happiness drain from her.

Walking briskly towards the yachts was Dexter — and at his side was a clearly angry Naval officer. Lara's heart sank.

What on earth was Sebastian doing here? He was supposed to be some-where in the Med!

5

'No Sport For A Woman'

Looking at the rigid set of Sebastian's body as he and Dexter marched towards the boats, Lara jumped up nervously.

If she wanted to avoid an angry confrontation in front of everyone, she'd have to move quickly.

'Thanks for the coffee, guys,' she said, 'I'll catch you all later.' She leaped on to the quay and hurried to meet the two men.

'Lara, I haven't issued an official pass for your fiancé because he assures me his visit is purely a short, personal one. For security reasons, please see that he leaves the competitors' area by ten o'clock tonight.' Dexter's tone left Lara in no doubt that he wasn't happy with her 'unofficial' visitor.

He turned and walked away, leaving her to face Sebastian.

Aware that they could be overheard by everyone on the boat, she kept her voice low.

'What are you doing here, Sebastian?' she asked as calmly as she could. 'I thought you were on a hush-hush exercise?'

'We had to put back into Gibraltar for some essential repairs and I managed to wangle a two-day pass. Can we go somewhere and talk?'

'There's the marina café,' she said. 'I'm told they do a mean hot chocolate. While we walk you can start explaining — beginning with why you told Dexter I was your fiancée.'

'It was the only way I could persuade him to let me see you. He seemed to think you wouldn't have time for visitors.'

'He was right. There's still loads to do.'

'You didn't seem very busy just now,' Sebastian pointed out peevishly.

'I only got here a couple of hours ago. The guys were just being friendly. So, what are you doing here?'

'I can't talk to you on the telephone. And you're not answering my e-mails,' Sebastian said.

'I couldn't bear the thought of not seeing you for six months, Lara. I simply wanted to talk to you face to face before it's too late.'

'Too late?'

Sebastian pushed open the café door and together they made their way to an empty table in a far corner.

'Too late?' Lara repeated. 'For what?'

A smile fleetingly touched Sebastian's lips as he took her hand in his.

'Lara, I love you. I really don't want to come over all heavy-handed, but this is no sport for a woman.' He waved his hand in the general direction of the marina.

'I've come to ask you to withdraw from the race.'

Lara stared at him in disbelief, pulling her hand away.

'I'm frightened for you.'

Lara took a deep breath.

'I'm frightened for me, too. But I've told you, Sebastian, I'm taking part in this race. And there's nothing you can say or do that will stop me.'

'You could at least have discussed it with me. I would have thought you'd care about how I felt.'

'I'm sorry.' Lara sighed. 'I should have talked to you before. But everything happened so quickly after Tom's accident there wasn't time. Besides, I guess I knew what your reaction would be.'

She ran her hands through her hair distractedly.

'Anyway, we're having a discussion now. Only it's not a discussion, is it? You want me to do what you want, not what I want. Can't you understand how important this race is to me?'

'It's too dangerous. Why can't you content yourself with doing smaller races? When we're married, we can go sailing together. I enjoy the sport as much as anyone.

'It's not as if I'm asking you to give up sailing altogether — just this race. Please, Lara — for my sake.'

'For your sake?' Lara repeated incredulously.

'Sebastian, this is the twenty-first century. Women make their own decisions, live their own lives.'

She took a deep breath.

'Who knows, the whole thing may scare me rigid and when I get back I won't want to go anywhere near another ocean-going yacht. I'll be ready to settle down, we'll get married and have lots of kids.'

Sebastian sighed.

'But what if it has the opposite effect? What if you want to do more and more competitive sailing? To tell you the truth, I'm not sure I want a wife who's prepared to take such risks.'

They both sat silently, each deep in their own thoughts as the waitress put their hot chocolates on the table.

Wasted Journey

Lara was the first to speak. She wanted to try to make him understand.

'Sebastian, I won't pull out of the race. There's too much at stake, both for me personally and because of the investment the yard has made in *Clotted Cream*.'

'I love you, Lara. Can't you see that I just don't want anything to happen to you? I couldn't bear to lose you.'

'There's more than one way to lose me, Sebastian, and emotional blackmail is a sure-fire one,' Lara retorted sharply.

She stirred an extra spoonful of sugar into her drink before looking directly at Sebastian.

'I'm really sorry you've had a wasted journey. I can only suggest you return to your ship and concentrate on your own life and career whilst I'm away for the next few months.' She paused.

'The separation will give us both time to think about what we really want.'

Sebastian shrugged his shoulders.

'So nothing I can say will make any difference?'

'No. It would have been nice to have sailed with your support and good wishes, but I'm going — with or without them.'

Sebastian put his hand lightly on her arm.

'I wish you all the luck in the world, Lara. I think you're going to need it.'

Without another word, he stood up and walked out of the café — and out of her life? Lara watched in silence, her emotions in turmoil.

Supper Date

Lara hadn't been exaggerating when she'd told Sebastian there was still a great deal to do before the race.

But it wasn't all work. As Dexter had predicted, there was a lot of partying, too.

The morning the engineer came to seal off *Clotted Cream*'s engine for the race, Dexter turned up.

'I wondered if you'd like a quick trip into Plymouth whilst Trevor does his stuff?'

'Yes, please. I'd been wondering how I'd get into town.'

'I'll meet you in the carpark in, what?' Dexter glanced at his watch. 'Ten minutes?'

If Lara had expected Dexter to mention Sebastian's visit on the short drive into town, she was disappointed. She briefly contemplated apologising for the incident, then dismissed the idea. Dexter had probably already forgotten about it.

Once in town she whizzed around, picking up some essential underwear and a couple of T-shirts. Finally she treated herself to a lipstick and some perfume.

Coming out of the large department store, she spotted Dexter emerging from the toy shop opposite, deep in conversation on his mobile.

He waved and crossed over, snapping his phone shut.

'Finished?' he asked.

Lara nodded.

'I've all the essentials for the Southern Ocean now!' She laughed.

'Well, here's another one.' He handed her a package.

'No, don't open it now,' he said quickly as she was about to pull the wrapping paper off. 'Wait till we get back.'

'Thanks.'

Dexter smiled.

'I was going to treat us to lunch, but something urgent's cropped up at the marina. Will you have supper with me tonight instead?'

'I'd like that.'

Once back, Dexter made straight for his office and Lara reached *Clotted Cream* in time to see Trevor leaving.

'You're now officially 'engineless',' he said, pointing out the seals he'd placed on the engine and the prop.

'It's wind power only for the next six months.'

Waiting for Dexter under a star-filled

sky early that evening, Lara began to wonder if he'd forgotten their supper date. Then she smiled as she finally saw him heading towards her.

'Hi. Sorry I'm late. I thought we'd walk down to the Barbican,' Dexter said. 'There's a good bistro down there.'

'Sounds great,' Lara said, picking up her jacket.

Conversation, as they walked, was about the race and boats in general. By the time they got to the bistro Dexter had Lara in stitches about an incident involving him and Tom a few years ago.

The laughter set the tone for an evening that passed all too quickly for Lara. It was midnight as Dexter helped her back on board *Clotted Cream* and jumped down into the cockpit himself.

'Would you like a coffee?' Lara offered, suddenly feeling shy at their closeness.

Dexter shook his head.

'No, thanks. But I do want to ask you something.'

Lara waited.

'Are you engaged to Sebastian?' he asked quietly.

'No.' Lara shook her head.

'In that case, I don't have to feel guilty about kissing you goodnight.' He gathered her into his arms and his lips met hers.

Determined

Back at the yard, life was settling into a new routine and Cassie was busy catching up on some of the things that had inevitably been pushed to one side.

All the new handrails were in place on the barge and Anna had helped Mai finish the decorating. There were just two weeks before the first clients for the sailing school were due.

The fact they still didn't have an instructor was a problem that Cassie knew she'd have to tackle once Lara had set sail.

Tom had completely taken over the

organisational side of the Round The World Alone race for Lara and everything seemed to be running smoothly.

Cassie knew he and Mai were desperate to get back to River View, but even when he was out of the wheelchair and on crutches it would be weeks before he could manage the spiral staircase there.

In the meantime he and Mai were making the best of living in Cassie's spare room.

As the weekend of the race approached, the main discussion at the yard concerned Tom. He was determined to go to Plymouth to see Lara off and badgered the doctor for permission until he finally said yes.

Doug had offered Tom a berth on his luxury yacht *Megabyte* for the weekend, which Mai had regretfully turned down on his behalf. He'd cope on board for a few hours, but any longer would pose problems. But at least he'd be there to see *Clotted Cream* sail over the start line.

Cassie and Anna had gratefully accepted Doug's offer. Despite her apprehension about what the coming months might bring, Cassie was looking forward to the weekend, to spending time with Lara before she left on her big adventure.

Good Luck Token

The part of the marina where all the competitors' yachts were berthed was heaving with people when Cassie and Anna arrived. However, with the passes that Dexter had arranged, they had no difficulty in finding their way to *Megabyte's* mooring. Doug welcomed them on board and his daughter Vanessa showed them to their cabin.

'Dad's arranged a small party for tonight,' she told them as she opened the cabin door. 'He's hoping you're free to join us.'

'That would be lovely,' Anna said, but Cassie didn't commit herself. She'd find out what Lara was doing first.

Having unpacked her small suitcase, Cassie went for a wander around the quay.

Lara was just finishing a TV interview when Cassie reached *Clotted Cream*.

'Hi, Mum,' she called out. 'Come on board and I'll make you a coffee.'

Cassie looked around the cabin that was to be Lara's home for the next six months, trying to imprint every little detail in her memory so she'd be able to bring it all to mind when she thought about her daughter in the coming weeks.

By necessity, the cabin was functional and businesslike, and Cassie smiled as she saw the pictures and mementoes of home Lara had pinned around the chart table. She couldn't help laughing when she peered into Lara's sleeping quarters and saw Fred Bear's head peeping out of the sleeping bag.

Fred Bear had been Lara's companion since Miles had given him to her for her first birthday. Since then he'd gone everywhere with her.

Today he had a companion of his own. A cuddly black and white Emperor penguin was alongside him.

Cassie picked up the toy.

'Love the penguin. Where did you get him?'

'Dexter gave him to me as a good luck token. He's called Nero,' Lara said. 'Isn't he gorgeous?'

'A very handsome fellow,' Cassie agreed, putting Nero back down beside Fred Bear.

Plenty Of Time

'Have you heard from Sebastian since his visit?' she asked quietly.

'Not a word. Not even one of his reproachful e-mails.'

'He's just worried about you, Lara.' Cassie looked at her daughter.

'He rang me, you know — after he left you.'

'And?'

'He was very upset. He said you didn't love him enough to do what he asked. I did try to tell him that loving someone doesn't give you control over them.'

'What did he say to that?'

'He muttered something about me sounding like you and hung up.'

There was a short silence.

'Did you ever ask Dad to stop sailing?' Lara asked eventually.

'No. It was his life.'

'Did Dad ever ask you to give up something he didn't approve of?'

Cassie shook her head.

'He never had cause to. I've never been the adventurous type. I just wanted to be with him.'

'Would you have done so if he'd asked?' Lara persisted.

'I don't know, love. It was a long time ago. Things were different.' Cassie paused.

Now was not the time to tell Lara that she'd loved Miles so much she'd have done anything he asked.

'You're doing what you want to do, Lara. Give it your best and enjoy it. Put all thoughts of Sebastian and marriage out of your mind. There will be plenty of time for that afterwards.'

'Mum, I need to tell you something in case . . . ' She hesitated. 'Sebastian's ring is in the top drawer of the cupboard in my room. Would you make sure he gets it back, if . . . ?'

Cassie interrupted quickly. She didn't want that thought put into words. She pulled Lara quickly to her and gave her a big hug.

'Of course, love. But nothing is going to happen. You're going to sail around the world and come back a heroine.'

'All Systems Go'

Saturday morning — race day — dawned grey but dry. A brisk easterly breeze was blowing, which promised good sailing for the yachts as they crossed the start line.

Cassie, standing on *Megabyte's* deck early that morning, sleepily took in the activity all around her. Having promised her parents, Bill and Liz, a full report of the weekend, she was determined to soak up the atmosphere.

Just then, Anna appeared at her side. 'Compliments of the chef. Breakfast will be on the upper deck in five minutes, madam,' she said, as she handed Cassie a welcome mug of tea.

'How do you feel?' she asked. 'Are you seeing Lara this morning before she's towed out?'

Cassie shook her head.

'No. She did ask if I wanted to go out with the crew, but I'm too much of a coward. Besides, I hate crying in public.' She took a deep breath.

'We said our goodbyes last night.'

There was a short silence before Cassie pointed along the quay.

'There's Tom and Mai. Doug said they were breakfasting on board.' She waved to her son and daughter-in-law.

Getting Tom and his wheelchair on

board proved more difficult than Doug had hopcd, but Dexter appeared in the nick of time. His extra strength was enough to propel Tom up the steep gangplank.

'Thanks, mate,' Tom said gratefully. 'Have you seen Lara this morning?'

Dexter nodded.

'She's fine and raring to go. The shore crew are on board, ready for the tow out. It's all systems go.'

Declining the offer to join them for breakfast, Dexter took his leave.

'I've to shepherd some VIPs to the launch in about ten minutes,' he explained.

As he turned to run down the gangway he smiled at Cassie.

'Don't spend the next weeks worrying. Lara will be OK. She'll be phoning you from Cape Town before you know it.'

While they were having breakfast, the crew slipped *Megabyte* from her moorings and slowly they began to make their way, with the flotilla of boats that was already building up, out into Plymouth Sound.

Several of the yachts were already in the start zone. They saw *Clotted Cream* being towed out and Lara gave them an excited wave before she and the crew began hoisting the mainsail.

As *Megabyte's* hull cut her way through the rough water there was an air of anticipation on board.

The large crowd of boats, intent on giving the racing fleet a good send off, was churning the sea into a jumble of mismatched swells, wakes and waves.

As the time drew nearer for the start of the race, everybody watched while the boats did some tactical sailing in a bid to secure a good position. Every skipper wanted to be first over the line when the gun went.

Lara's Good Start

For Cassie, one of the worst moments came when the support boat drew up alongside *Clotted Cream* and she saw the crew all hugging Lara goodbye, before climbing over the rails and leaving her on board alone.

Surreptitiously, Cassie wiped a tear away and hoped that nobody had noticed.

With only ten minutes to go now, she knew that nothing would stop Lara from crossing the start line and she watched with mounting anxiety as her daughter manoeuvred *Clotted Cream* into what she hoped would be a good position.

The split second silence that followed the firing of the start gun was drowned by the raucous sound of hundreds of foghorns being blasted simultaneously. Cassie held her breath, watching Lara tack, come round and race over the line in third position.

'Yes!' Tom shouted, his fist striking the air with delight. 'Good start, Lara.'

Then his voice broke and a sob almost escaped his lips. He was delighted for his sister. But he couldn't help the bitter jealousy that suddenly welled up inside him. It should have been him sailing out on the adventure of a lifetime.

He turned away, unable to watch as the fleet sailed off, becoming mere specks in the distance.

'Be careful, Lara, be careful.' Cassie closed her eyes and muttered the words over and over again to herself.

'Cassie — champagne to celebrate Lara's good start?'

Startled out of her reverie, Cassie turned and accepted the glass Doug was offering her. As she took it a mobile phone began to ring.

Doug gave the toast, 'To Lara and *Clotted Cream*,' and everybody raised their glasses.

Cassie had barely taken a sip when Tom spoke.

'Text message for you, Mum.' He handed her his mobile phone.

Just to say thanks, Mum. Couldn't be doing this without your blessing. Have left u a present with Dexter. Love u, Lara.

Cassie, despite her promise to herself not to cry in public, promptly burst into tears.

Frightened

Because of the large number of boats making their way back into Plymouth after the start of the race, it was a couple of hours before *Megabyte* was able to tie up at her mooring.

Tom was clearly tired and Cassie was relieved to see Dexter waiting on the quay, ready to give them a hand getting him ashore.

Once Tom and Mai left, Cassie and Anna said their goodbyes to Doug and Vanessa and made their way to the car.

'Want me to drive?' Anna offered.

'No, I'm fine, thanks,' Cassie said. 'I'm quite looking forward to the journey back. I thought we might stop for supper somewhere.'

'Good idea.'

It was nearly ten o'clock before

Cassie reached the lane that ran down to the boatyard. She was just making the turn when her headlights caught something at the side of the road and she slammed the brakes on.

'There's somebody in the hedge!'

Frightened, Cassie and Anna looked at each other. The boatyard was three miles down the track. Should they go for help or investigate it themselves?

Winding the car window down a fraction, Cassie listened to the night sounds, trying to hear if there was anybody about.

An owl hooted in the distance. Nothing out of the ordinary.

Cassie slowly backed the car up until the headlights illuminated the hedge.

She and Anna got out of the car and cautiously made their way towards the figure. Curled up in the hedge, eyes watching them fearfully, was a dog. As they got closer she slowly rose to her feet and waited.

Both Cassie and Anna breathed a sigh of relief. They could cope with this.

'Poor old thing,' Cassie said, stretching out a hand to stroke the dog. 'Do you think she's been hit by a car?'

'I don't think so,' Anna said, carefully running her hands over the dog's body. 'I think she's either been dumped or she's a stray. Look how thin she is.'

'Come on, let's get her into the car,' Cassie said. 'We can't leave her here. I'll take her home for the night and call the RSPCA tomorrow.'

The dog looked at Cassie and a tongue cautiously licked her hand. It was as if she sensed Cassie was to be her saviour.

Once back home, Cassie opened a tin of stewing steak, which the dog ate gratefully, before having a long drink from the bowl of water Cassie put down for her.

The dog's eyes followed her every movement and, as Cassie made her up a bed out of some old cushions, she nuzzled gently at Cassie's ear.

'Hey, that tickles.' Cassie laughed.

The dog leaned against her and

Cassie absently stroked the soft head.

'That should do you for the night,' she said finally. 'I'll see you in the morning. Everything is going to be all right. I'll make sure you go to a good home.'

The dog's eyes looked trustingly into Cassie's and she gave a very slight wag of her tail before heaving a deep sigh and settling on the cushions.

Once in bed, Cassie said a prayer for Lara's safety, turned off the light and went to sleep.

In her dreams that night, she was running alongside the river trying to catch an elusive figure in the distance. A familiar-looking dog bounded happily at her side.

When she woke in the morning, the dog was curled up at her feet.

6

'She Can't Stay Here'

'What are you going to call her?' Anna asked the next morning when she brought Cassie a cup of tea and saw the dog on the bed.

'I'm not keeping her,' Cassie said. 'First thing this morning I'll ring round and see if anyone's reported her missing. If not, I'll take her to the animal sanctuary across town.'

The dog looked up at the sound of Cassie's voice, before deliberately snuggling in closer and uttering a deep sigh.

'Oh, yes?' Anna laughed.

'She can't stay here,' Cassie said. 'It's out of the question.'

'Why?' Anna asked. 'You like dogs — and the feeling is clearly mutual! At least think about it.'

Three hours later, Cassie finally put

the phone down, having drawn a blank with all the vets, police and animal sanctuaries in the area. The dog hadn't been microchipped and nobody within a fifty-mile radius had any record of a lurcher cross bitch being reported missing.

Cassie looked across the room to where the dog was sleeping peacefully, stretched out alongside Tom as he worked on the computer. As Cassie watched her, she opened her eyes, her gaze full of trust.

'Why don't you get some fresh air?' Tom suggested. 'Have a think. Take the dog.'

Cassie realised he'd studiously avoided saying the word 'walk', but the dog was on her feet, looking at her expectantly.

Cassie took the short cut down through the boatyard path. The dog waited patiently at her side as she unlocked the gate in the perimeter fence, before bounding excitedly down to the river's edge.

'Come on girl, this way.' Cassie

began to head upstream.

Walking past River View, Cassie wondered when Tom and Mai would be able to move back in. It would be several weeks yet, she suspected.

Anna would probably have settled into her new house by that time too.

When they all moved out she'd be on her own. She couldn't count on Lara wanting to live at home again once the race was over.

Cassie sighed. Everybody's lives were changing, and she was determined not to miss the boat this time.

A glimmer of an idea began to take shape in her mind.

There were a few boats on the river, including the harbour master's official launch with James at it's helm. He waved as he passed and shouted a greeting that was mainly carried on the wind.

As she waved back, she glanced down at the dog who was gently nuzzling her hand.

'What is it girl?' Cassie said stroking

her. 'I like you, too. We're going to have to find you a proper name aren't we? We can't keep calling you 'the dog' or 'girl'.'

Realising what she'd just said, Cassie laughed out loud. Her subconscious had made the decision. The dog was staying.

'So how about Willow?' She shook her head. 'No. Tess? Honey?'

Undecided, Cassie studied the dog for several minutes before inspiration struck.

'I know. You were on your own when I found you, and Lara has gone off alone. I'm going to call you Solo.'

Solo looked at her, ears cocked, licked her hand as if in agreement and then bounded off to chase an imaginary rabbit.

'I'm Pregnant!'

When they finally returned to the boatyard, Doug was coming out of the

157

office. 'Hello,' he greeted Cassie. 'I've been having a word with Bill about doing some maintenance work on *Megabyte* whilst I'm away.' He glanced at her.

'I was hoping you'd have dinner with me one evening, but I'm afraid it will have to wait until I get back from Scotland.'

'I'll look forward to it,' Cassie said. 'When do you leave?'

'First thing in the morning. I'll be away for two to three weeks.'

'Why don't you join us for dinner tonight?' Cassie said impulsively. 'It would give me a chance to say thank you for your generous hospitality in Plymouth. Half-past seven, OK?'

'Perfect. I'll see you then,' Doug said.

Tom and Mai were waiting for her in the kitchen when she got back. Cassie was suddenly seized with apprehension.

'What's wrong?' she asked.

'Absolutely nothing,' Tom replied.

He was holding Mai's hand, and a big smile spread over his face.

'We wanted you to be the first to know.'

'I'm pregnant!' Mai said. 'The doctor confirmed it this morning.'

'You're going to be a granny!' Tom exclaimed at the same time.

'Oh congratulations!' Cassie kissed Mai and hugged Tom.

'That's wonderful news. We must celebrate this evening,' she added.

'Incidentally, I've asked Doug to join us.'

'It'll be quite a party.' Tom grinned. 'Dexter rang to say he'd call in on his way back to London. I invited him for dinner — and offered him a bed for the night too.'

'Any news from Lara?' Cassie asked.

'She sent an e-mail. I printed it out. I thought you might want to keep them.'

'Good idea,' Cassie said, picking up the print-out.

First twenty-four hours at sea have been fine. We are well on our way to Finisterre. Weather forecast is reasonable, so hopefully it won't be too rough. Love, Lara.

'Another day or two and she'll be down around the Azores, won't she?' Cassie said thoughtfully.

Tom glanced at her, his expression one of concern. He knew only too well how his mother felt about that particular stretch of ocean.

A Present From Lara

When Dexter arrived that evening, he was full of the latest news about the race.

'Lara is fine,' he reassured Cassie, before telling them the story of an unfortunate competitor who'd got caught in the edge of a weather system off the coast of France and lost his mast.

'He's had to put into a French port for repairs. Hopefully he'll be able to rejoin the fleet next week and still make it to Cape Town within the time limit,' Dexter said.

Dinner that evening was a good-humoured meal with much laughter and lively conversation. In a pause between courses Dexter asked how bookings for the barge were going.

'Trickling in nicely,' Tom said. 'The only problem is we still haven't found a temporary instructor yet.' He glanced at his mother.

'I've put an ad on the Yacht Club noticeboard and James is asking around,' Cassie said defensively. 'Somebody will turn up. But if they don't . . . ' She paused. 'I'll do it.'

'Thanks, Mum,' Tom said gratefully. 'Problem solved.'

'Um, actually, I don't think it is,' Dexter said unexpectedly.

'Cassie, I should have given you this earlier.' He handed her a large white envelope.

'It's a present Lara asked me to give you.'

Cassie slit open the envelope.

'Do you know what it is?'

Dexter nodded.

'I helped arrange it.'

Cassie was speechless as she took out

of the envelope a hotel brochure and a return ticket to Cape Town.

'Lara would like you to be on the quay when she sails in,' Dexter said. 'She also reckoned you'd quite like it, too! The hotel booking is for a week.'

Cassie was stunned.

'But I can't go. I've just agreed to take on the instructing. And what about Solo? And things here?'

'I think I can help with the sailing,' Doug offered.

'One of my crew on *Megabyte* is a qualified dinghy instructor. I'd be more than happy for him to help out whilst you're in South Africa.'

'And I'll still be here,' Anna said. 'I can fill in for you wherever I'm needed.'

'Don't worry about Solo. Tom and I will take care of her until you get back,' Mai put in.

'There you go, Mum. No excuses. In two weeks' time you can jet off to Cape Town to welcome Lara ashore,' Tom said.

Lara's Journal

Wednesday 15th.
I've decided to keep a private journal as well as my official log but, five days into the race, this is the first opportunity I've had to write it up.

Sailing with the fleet out of Plymouth Sound was awesome. So many people had come to see us off. I felt very insignificant, but proud to be a part of the whole pageant.

Waving goodbye was very emotional but I managed to keep the tears at bay until nobody could see me.

I felt so sorry for Tom. Clotted Cream is his boat, after all. It must have been difficult for him, seeing me set off in a race that he should have been doing.

Getting down channel was hair-raising — there was so much traffic in the shipping lanes, but at least we got past the Lizard in daylight.

There were three of us setting much the same course the first afternoon and evening and we all did a lot of tactical sailing. Overnight, though, we altered our courses slightly and by dawn I was alone.

Very excited by the telephone conversation with Race HQ this morning. They told me I'm currently lying in second position. I know, I know, it's early days.

I've had several e-mails since setting sail — one from Mum, thanking me for the ticket and looking forward to seeing me in Cape Town.

Dexter sent me an e-mail, too, telling me to take care and sail safely. He promised he'd be waiting with Mum in South Africa. Still no word from Sebastian, but I didn't really expect to hear. I'll e-mail him in a few days just to see how he is and to try to keep things on a reasonably friendly footing.

By the time I got to Finisterre the wind had increased as a front came through. It certainly lived up to its rough reputation — freezing wind and fine driving rain. I know, though, I'll encounter worse conditions down in the Southern Ocean so I'd better get used to it.

We came through the front overnight and this morning I was rewarded with the sight of a group of dolphins leaping and swimming and joyfully escorting me for a few miles.

Oh, I do so love being at sea.

Tonight the weather is much calmer and everything on board is fine. The moon is out and the stars are shining. Robbie Williams is playing on the CD and I'm going to have a bowl of pasta and the last of my bananas for supper before having a snooze.

Tomorrow I'll be that much further from the Azores. I'm trying not to think about Dad, but every now and again a shudder goes through me when the waves are unexpectedly noisy against the hull or some debris floats past.

I'll be glad when I'm further down off the coast of Africa. I'll have left the ghosts behind then.

Open For Business

'Jibe!' Cassie shouted from her position at the tiller. The two teenagers ducked and made for the other side of the dinghy as the boom swung the mainsail across and the small boat changed tack.

'Good. Well done. Now, I think it's Wayne's turn to take us back to the barge.'

Just three days into their holiday, the boys were already getting the hang of sailing. Cassie was pleased with the way they'd responded to her lessons and was quietly proud of herself.

The first week of the barge being open for business was going well. To Cassie's unspoken relief the party of five teenagers had cancelled and the Rogers family had taken their place at the last minute, with just the two boys needing tuition.

Wayne and Terry's parents loved their accommodation on board and were delighted with the freedom that the boys' sailing lessons gave them.

After Wayne had brought the dinghy alongside the barge to the enthusiastic applause of his proud parents, Cassie had a word with Mai. She was in the small galley preparing dinner for the guests.

'How are you feeling? Are you coping all right with the cooking?'

'I'm fine. Not even too queasy — unless I try to fry onions! By the way, James called. Something about next week?'

'He's been trying to get tickets for a concert. I'll ring him when I get indoors.'

When Cassie got back to the house Tom was busy on the computer. Solo was lying at his feet, her favourite place when Cassie wasn't around. The moment she spotted her mistress, though, Solo jumped up and gave her an excited welcome.

'Has James left a message for me, Tom?' Cassie asked.

'He just wanted you to know he's got the tickets for the concert next Thursday.'

'I leave on Friday morning,' Cassie

pointed out. 'I was hoping to spend the evening here with you and Mai.'

'Look on it as an early start to your holiday. We'll have a family evening on Wednesday.'

Tom changed the subject.

'Lara's just posted a copy of her first article for the newspaper on the web-site. It's good.' He sounded surprised.

'How close to the Canaries is she now?' Cassie asked.

'Almost there. She'll be picking up the Trade Winds any day now on her way down to the Equator.'

Involuntarily, Cassie found herself letting a deep breath go. Lara was safely past the Azores. The dreaded anniversary of Miles's fatal accident had come and gone with nothing untoward to mark it. She could relax slightly.

'I think I'll take Solo for a walk before dinner. Honestly, it's years since I've had so much exercise. It must be good for me, I suppose.'

'If you're going along the river path, could you pop into River View and pick up some CDs for me?' Tom asked. 'I keep forgetting to ask Mai. The key's on my beside table. Thanks.

'And don't worry, I'll listen to them on my headphones. I won't blast the place with noise!'

When Cassie got back to the house, Tom and Mai were deep in conversation with an excited Anna.

'They've finally accepted my offer for Glebe House. Two months and it will be mine,' she told Cassie.

'I'm so pleased for you,' Cassie said. 'We'll miss having you here, but it'll make a lovely home. Besides, it's not too far away.'

'There are a couple of auctions coming up next month. Will you come with me when you get back?

'Oh, it's going to be such fun decorating and furnishing.' Anna smiled happily.

Cassie's Proposition

The next ten days were busy ones for Cassie. In between giving sailing lessons she had to organise things for when she was away and — a major problem — find enough clothes for her holiday!

Anna was a great help, not only offering to drive her to the station, but raiding her own wardrobe and lending Cassie a few choice items.

Finally, everything was done. Cassie's suitcase was packed, with the exception of her evening dress, which would go in after tonight's concert date with James.

Gazing critically at her reflection in the full-length mirror, Cassie thought she looked reasonably presentable, if a trifle boring.

She was about to fix her pearl stud earrings in place, when she stopped and went through to Lara's bedroom. Lara often borrowed bits and pieces from her and Cassie knew she wouldn't mind her rummaging through her more modern jewellery.

The dangly silver earrings she found were perfect. With the addition of a scarlet pashmina, the whole outfit was transformed. Finally satisfied with her appearance, Cassie made her way downstairs. She had a proposition to put to Tom and Mai before James arrived.

'You look great, Mum,' Tom said.

'Thanks.' Cassie smiled.

'I want to ask you two to think about something while I'm away, and there won't be time in the morning.'

Tom and Mai looked puzzled.

'How would you feel about swapping houses with me?' She held a hand up to silence them before they could say anything.

'No, hear me out. You're going to be living here for the next couple of months anyway, until Tom is out of the wheelchair. And when the baby arrives, River View will be too small. It makes much more sense for you to make this place your permanent home.'

'But why would you want to live on your own in River View?' Mai asked.

'Because I'm nearly fifty years old and I've never lived on my own. I just feel it's about time for me to take charge of my life. Living in River View would be the first step.

'You're going to need more room with the baby, and this place will be Tom's eventually anyway.'

As Cassie heard James's car drive into the yard she picked up her bag.

'Promise me you'll think about it while I'm away. We can have a proper discussion when I get back,' she said.

'Music And Romance'

The concert James had tickets for was being held in the grounds of a nearby stately home. The advertising posters promised *an evening of music and romance in the spirit of yester-year*.

Parking the car, James and Cassie joined the crowds that were walking towards the wide expanse of lawn where the stage had been set. Huge torch candles lit the way, while smaller ones set amongst the trees shimmered in the twilight like fireflies.

'It's as if we're stepping back in time,' Cassie whispered. 'All these people in period costume — I feel as though I'm an extra in some historical film.'

'Cassie, the way you look tonight, you're the star,' James said, his expression one of genuine admiration.

As the sun finally set, throwing golden streaks across the darkening sky behind the manor house, a solo flautist began to play, gradually teasing the other orchestra instruments into life. Cassie closed her eyes and allowed herself to float with the music.

James held her hand in his, their fingers entwined, letting go only occasionally to applaud the musicians.

The concert came to an end far too

soon for Cassie. Turning to James, she sighed.

'Thank you so much, James. That was a truly magical experience.'

He leaned forward and kissed her gently on the cheek.

'The evening's not over yet,' he said. 'I've booked a table for supper. So if m'lady will accompany me?' He took hold of her hand again.

Together, they followed a footman down a path that wove its way through formal gardens before finishing at the foot of a flight of grand stone steps leading up to the huge oak doors of the house.

Within minutes they were seated at a table for two under the candle-burning chandelier of the Tudor dining-room.

'I feel as if I've been transported back to the sixteenth century,' Cassie whispered, looking around her at the tapestries and costumes.

'I can scarcely believe that tomorrow I'm getting on a plane and jetting off to South Africa. This world seems so real.'

A trio was softly playing and already there was a couple swaying gently together on the small area of dance-floor at the far end of the room.

'Shall we join them?' James asked.

As his arms went around her and they began to move in time to the slow old-fashioned music, Cassie felt a twinge of misgiving. She hoped that James wasn't going to try to take their relationship beyond friendship. She'd only just come to terms with the fact that she'd been letting life pass her by. She didn't want to hurt him, but she had to find out what she really wanted, before becoming involved in a serious relationship with anyone.

James's next words confirmed her fears.

'Cassie, I know you're only going away for a week, and I haven't forgotten that you once told me it was just friendship you were looking for, but I wanted this to be a special evening.' He paused.

'The first of many for us. I want to be more than your friend. Will you think about us whilst you're away?'

James drew her firmly towards him, his lips gently caressing her cheek.

'I've fallen in love with you, Cassie.'

7

Lara's Journal

Saturday 1st.
At 3 a.m. yesterday, Clotted Cream and I were bathed in moonlight as we crossed the Equator. I'm very proud of myself — I managed to set the video and capture my celebration on tape!

It feels really good to have covered this distance, although it's getting harder with each day.

My hands aren't helping. They're a mass of tiny salt blisters, which are very painful.

The Equator is renowned for being a temperamental place to sail and I've been trying to keep as far to the west as possible, hoping to pick up a steadier breeze. For the last few days that ploy has worked, but now the winds are getting stronger and the waves bigger.

The autopilot was struggling as *Clotted Cream* hurtled down, riding the waves, so I've spent a lot of time at the helm — wonderfully exhilarating!

Unfortunately, one of the results of all these strong winds and fast sailing has been a broken batten in the sail.

When the wind finally abated and the rain came, the only way round it was to lower the mainsail and replace the batten. It took me ten minutes to re-hoist the sail, but eventually it was up and we were on the move again after a delay of nearly two hours. It could have been worse.

Rewarded myself for all the hard work with the last of the caramel chocolate bars. They're top of my shopping list for Cape Town.

The rest of my food supplies seem to be holding out well, though I'm looking forward to some fresh fruit and veggies.

After my daily chat with Race HQ this morning I typed my weekly bulletin for the newspaper and e-mailed it. With a bit of luck I'll be doing the next one from a berth in Cape Town.

I can't believe that I'm still in second place. Hopefully I can hang on to it. I don't think there's much chance of me catching up with Colin on Flight Of The Seagull. He's nearly two hundred miles in front. My biggest worry is the third place boat, World Wanderer. She's only about seventy miles behind me. I could easily drop a place in the next week if I don't keep pushing hard.

The generator is on, charging all the electrics. Seems to be extra noisy tonight for some reason. (Must check that with Tom.)

Thoughts Of Home

Anna was driving Cassie to the station where she'd catch the train to the airport.

'Is everything OK?' she asked her friend. 'You look a bit strained.'

Cassie nodded.

'I'm fine. *Just* a little nervous. I never did like flying.'

'You'll have a marvellous time in Cape Town. Don't worry about anything back here. *Just* concentrate on enjoying yourself with Lara.'

Cassie tried to follow Anna's advice, but by the time she boarded the flight to Cape Town, thoughts of home were still occupying her mind. She could only hope she'd done everything necessary to keep the place ticking over for the week she was away.

As the air hostess arrived with her meal tray, Cassie remembered last night's supper with James and their conversation after he'd confessed he'd fallen in love with her.

James was a lovely man, a very dear friend, but Cassie wasn't ready for anything more.

Once back at their table, she'd steeled herself to tell him the truth.

'I've had a wonderful evening, James, and it will always be a special *memory* for me.' She paused *before* continuing.

'You know I like you a lot. And I look upon you as a good friend — the best. But I'm not sure about love.'

James was silent for some time, then he sighed.

'Cassie, your friendship is very precious to me and I don't want to lose it. I had hoped it might be growing into more on your part but clearly I've spoken too soon. Let's not spoil what, as you say, has been a special evening, through my foolishness.'

He reached across the table and gently stroked her hand.

'I just want you to know that I do love you, and if you ever feel you can love me in return, I'll be waiting.' Now, as she looked out at the carpet of clouds beneath the plane as they sped towards the Cape, Cassie's thoughts returned to the present. She was determined to enjoy this holiday. Hopefully, when she returned home she'd be fighting fit and ready to get her life in order.

Twelve hours later, as an exhausted

Cassie walked into the arrivals lounge of Cape Town International Airport, she was surprised to see Dexter waiting for her.

'This is a lovely surprise, Dexter. I didn't expect to see you until tomorrow.'

'I thought a friendly face might be appreciated — and a helping hand to get you to your hotel. I'll not be able to stay for long, though. I've got some organising to do for tomorrow. The first boat is due to cross the line in about twenty-four hours.'

He shook his head in answer to Cassie's unspoken question.

'No, sorry. It's not Lara, but last I heard she was still in second place.

'Now, come on, let's find a taxi and get you into Cape Town.'

The hotel Lara had booked her into was by the waterfront.

'I've reserved a table for dinner,' Dexter told her. 'I'll see you later.' He headed off, leaving the porter to show her to her room.

'A View You'll Never Forget'

Situated on the top floor of the spacious hotel, the twin-bedded room had a view out over the harbour. There was a magnificent arrangement of flowers on a low table at the foot of one of the beds.

It wasn't until after she'd had a reviving shower that Cassie noticed the card nestling in between the tight red buds of the roses. She read the message.

Have a wonderful time. Looking forward to our dinner on your return. Regards, Doug.

Cassie put the card in her bag — a reminder to say thank you when she got home.

Refreshed by the shower and a couple of hours' sleep, she made her way down to the foyer to wait for Dexter.

Outside, the quay was preparing for the evening's entertainment. Neon lights were flashing on and off, table candles were lit at various harbour-side restaurants and music was beginning to infiltrate the night air.

A schooner, moored at the far end of the harbour, was dressed from stern to bow with flags and small lights that added their reflections to others in the rippling water as the boat tugged gently at its anchor.

Above it all, the silhouette of Table Mountain could be seen against the darkening night sky. Wisps of gossamer-thin mist teased Cassie's view of it.

'It's a view you'll never forget seeing,' Dexter said as he appeared at her side. 'Shall we go?'

Companionably, they walked along the waterfront. The restaurant he'd chosen was well placed for watching the comings and goings of both boats and people and Cassie was soon soaking up Cape Town's unique harbour-side atmosphere.

★　★　★

The next day, after a good night's sleep, Cassie set out for the yacht club. Dexter had told her *Flight Of The Seagull* should cross the finish line some time in the afternoon. He'd given her a pass for the reception area.

Once inside the club, Cassie could feel the buzz of excitement in the air. As she stood there uncertainly, searching for Dexter in the crowd, another official came over and glanced at her pass.

'Ah, Mrs Lewis — Little Lara's mother.' He smiled at her.

'Welcome. I think your team are out on the terrace.' He turned, clearly expecting her to follow him.

Team? In the midst of all the excitement, Cassie had forgotten that the shore crew would be in Cape Town waiting for Lara. In fact, they'd be following her all around the world.

At the finish of every leg they'd go over the yacht and get her ready for the next stage of the voyage.

'What's the latest news of Lara?' she asked.

It was the Rule of Thumb technician who answered her.

'She's still in second place, about twelve hours behind Colin, but she's got a problem with her generator which may have slowed her down.

'Still, with luck she should be here in the early hours.'

'There's nothing seriously wrong, is there? You would tell me, wouldn't you?' Cassie asked anxiously.

'I've spoken to her and so has Tom. She's fine. She just wants this leg of the race over.'

Cassie accepted the offer of a cup of coffee from a passing waiter. A few more hours and she could breathe a sigh of relief. Lara would be here.

'Cassie? Cassie Lewis?'

Hearing her name, Cassie turned, her eyes widening in disbelief.

'Becky?'

When the two women finally disentangled themselves from their spontaneous hug, they stood back and looked at each in amazement.

For Cassie it was like turning the clock back twenty years. Becky, wife of Miles's best friend and rival, Trevor Thomas, was as glamorous as ever.

Once upon a time, she and Becky had been great friends and had spent a lot of time together in various harbours whilst their husbands were off sailing. After Miles's death, however, Cassie had deliberately lost touch with the couple. Becky and Trevor were too painful a reminder of what she'd lost.

Now she looked at her old friend with affection and regretted those lost years.

'What are you doing here?' Cassie asked.

'We live here. It's been about seven years now — ever since Trev gave up racing professionally. He runs his own charter business, but still gets involved with yacht racing whenever he can. He's skippering the official boat out to meet Colin.'

Becky looked across at the growing

crowd of spectators lining the quay, the small boats setting off to escort a triumphant *Flight Of The Seagull* to her temporary berth.

'I can't believe Lara is grown up enough to be taking part,' she went on. 'When I saw her name on the competitors' list I promised myself I would meet her. I didn't dare hope you'd be here to welcome her ashore.' Becky sighed contentedly.

'Promise me we won't lose touch again? Oh, Cassie, we've got so much to catch up on. Come on, let's find a seat and talk about the old days, before the place erupts with champagne for the winner.'

Frenzied Barking

'Anna and I are off out with Solo. Will you be OK for a while?' Mai asked.

Tom nodded, concentrating on the computer screen.

'I'm trying to find some more info for

Lara. She's still having problems with the generator.'

'OK. We'll leave you to it.' Mai took Solo's lead off its peg.

As she and Anna made their way down through the yard, Mai glanced across at the barge, now secure on its mooring in the river.

This new venture seemed to be going well, in spite of the initial problems. Justin, the *Megabyte* crew member Doug had lent them while Cassie was away, had turned out to be a good instructor.

'How's the morning sickness?' Anna asked as Mai let Solo off her lead. The dog bounded away to sniff her way along the path.

'Better every day,' Mai said. 'Which is a huge relief. Have you had any more news on your house?'

'The survey was done yesterday. A couple more weeks to completion and then the builders can go in and sort the bathroom and install the Aga.'

'Has Cassie mentioned her idea of

swapping houses with Tom and me?' Mai asked casually.

Anna nodded.

'Yes. She's very keen on the idea.'

'She hasn't just suggested it because she knows it would make life easier for us?'

'Definitely not,' Anna said firmly. 'Cassie wants to do something she's never done before — live alone, with no responsibility for anyone but herself. And Solo, of course.' She laughed as the dog came racing back to them with a large stick for them to throw.

'How do you feel about the idea anyway?' She looked at Mai.

'It would be great. Tom should be out of the wheelchair soon and the stairs there are a lot easier for him to manage. We could have a proper nursery, too.'

Sudden frenzied barking from Solo brought the conversation to an abrupt end as Mai and Anna began to run towards her.

A teenage boy was trying to free a small wooden boat from the mud flat on the river's edge. An outboard motor fixed lopsidedly to the boat's stern looked in danger of falling off. As Solo continued to bark at the boy, he kicked out at her.

'Hey, stop that!' Anna and Mai both yelled together.

'The dog attacked me. Dangerous dogs are supposed to be muzzled.'

'She's not dangerous. You must have done something to upset her,' Anna snapped.

'Solo, come here.' She called the dog. With a last loud warning bark at the boy, Solo reluctantly did as she was told and Mai quickly clipped on her lead. Solo continued to utter low-throated growls as they walked away, leaving the boy struggling to get the boat into the water.

Back at the yard, they told Tom about the incident.

'He was probably doing some illicit fishing.' Tom shrugged.

'I don't know, Tom,' Anna said. 'He looked pretty shifty to me. And Solo definitely didn't like him.'

'Well, if you're worried, mention it to James. He usually knows which rogues are out and about on the river. Right now, though, I've got enough to worry about.' He looked at them steadfastly.

'I've lost contact with Lara. And so has Race HQ.'

'A Long Night'

Flight of the Seagull had sailed into Cape Town to a rapturous welcome before the news filtered through that contact had been lost with Lara and *Clotted Cream*.

Around her, the noise of the celebrations faded into the background as a shocked Cassie tried to take in what Dexter was telling her.

'Cassie, please don't worry. We know her position as of twelve hours ago when she was fine and making good time.

'We also know she's been having

problems with her generator. More than likely that's what has caused the communication problem.'

Cassie looked at him numbly, willing him to be speaking the truth.

'Right now, Race HQ is contacting the boat in third position to ask if he has seen her. As soon as we have any news you'll be told.

'It could be some time before we hear anything, though,' Dexter continued. 'Why don't you go back to the hotel and get some rest?'

'I'd rather wait here,' Cassie began to protest, when Becky interrupted.

'I'll drive you. I've got my mobile and the moment there's any news Trev or Dexter will phone. We can be back here in minutes.'

Dexter looked at her gratefully.

'Honestly, Cassie, nothing is going to happen for a few hours.'

Once back at the hotel, Becky insisted on ordering some sandwiches and a pot of coffee from room service.

'Come on, Cassie, you need to eat

something. It's going to be a long night.'

But Cassie was too wound up to eat or drink a thing.

Becky's prophecy of a long night proved to be true. It was gone two o'clock when her mobile phone rang.

Cassie, lying on the bed with her eyes closed, feigning sleep, was immediately on her feet, staring fearfully at her friend.

'Thanks, Trev. I'll tell her.' Becky looked at Cassie.

'They've had a sighting of Lara. There's still been no contact, but she appears to be sailing hard and, on her current course, is about three hours away from Cape Town.'

'What else?'

'The sighting was made by the yacht in third position, *World Wanderer*. He's rapidly gaining on her and there's a chance that Lara will lose her second position.'

'So long as she's safe.' Cassie's reaction was instinctive.

'Dexter has arranged for you to go out in the launch when we get back to the yacht club and escort *Clotted Cream* into her berth,' Becky told her.

Cassie immediately picked up her yellow waterproofs.

'Let's go,' she said.

As they drove back towards the yacht club, Cassie was amazed at the number of people making their way along the waterfront.

'They'll have heard of Lara's problems and be determined to give her a proper welcome to Cape Town, even if it is the middle of the night.'

Dexter was waiting for them, Trev and Colin, the winning skipper, with him.

'Cassie, we've got an estimated time of five o'clock for Lara crossing the finish, so we plan to leave here in about an hour.'

Now she knew Lara was within sight of the coastline Cassie felt the nervous tension of the past few hours slipping away.

She struggled into her waterproofs and headed off with the others down to the boat. On the way, Cassie asked Dexter about the yacht which had reported sighting Lara.

'Is he still gaining on her?'

Dexter shook his head.

'No, she's managing to hold on to her lead, but the wind a couple of miles offshore is very fickle. She's going to lose speed the closer she gets to the finish line. But then, so is *World Wanderer*.'

There was a discernible hum of excitement aboard the flotilla of boats going out to the finish line.

As Trev said to Cassie as they took off into the night, 'To have two yachts still racing in such close quarters for second place after nearly seven thousand miles is almost unheard of.'

It was Colin who spotted the first sails.

'There's one of them,' he shouted, his binoculars with their night sight trained on the distant sea.

'It's *World Wanderer*.'

He scanned the sea again while Cassie's heart began to pound. Where was Lara?

Tears

Half a minute passed before Colin handed Cassie the binoculars and pointed out the direction in which she should look. Lara was coming in on a different course.

Everyone held their breath, wondering which skipper had chosen the better option.

As the sky began to lighten and dawn approached, *Clotted Cream* drew closer, her mainsail taking full advantage of the available breeze. Finally, she was close enough for Cassie to see the small figure of her daughter standing in the cockpit.

Cassie felt the tell-tale pinprick of tears starting in her eyes. She knew Lara would be desperate to finish before *World Wanderer*, whereas she was just pleased to have her daughter complete this first leg safely.

'Wind's died,' Trev observed.

Lara's sail began to flap and she quickly tacked in an effort to find some air movement. The next few minutes were nerve-racking as *Clotted Cream* wallowed in the sea, tantalisingly close to the finish line, and her rival sailed closer.

Then, at the moment the sky turned pale pink with the dawn, *Clotted Cream* found an elusive breeze.

Two minutes later the gun rang out as she crossed the line to a tumultuous welcome. Lara had done it. She was second. *World Wanderer* followed her in six minutes later to an equally enthusiastic reception.

Flares were set off, boat hooters sounded, cameras flashed and champagne corks popped. The shore crew boarded *Clotted Cream* and took control of her as she was towed into port.

Lara, punching the air with delight, was overjoyed to see Cassie in the launch.

'Come on board, Mum!' she cried.

By the time Cassie had clambered on to the deck of *Clotted Cream*, the tears were flowing freely from both mother and daughter. As they made the short trip into the harbour Cassie struggled to get her emotions under control and asked Lara why she'd lost contact in the last twenty-four hours.

'The generator packed up and unfortunately I'd forgotten to charge my batteries fully the night before. The only thing I could do was to switch everything off so there would be enough power to work the autopilot every hour while I had a catnap.

'Thank goodness it happened at the end of the leg. No autopilot means no sleep.'

'Well Done!'

Once the yacht was tied up in her allocated berth Dexter came on board to congratulate Lara.

'Well done, Lara,' he said, giving her a warm hug, holding her tight for several seconds.

Cassie was amused to see that Lara wasn't averse to staying in his arms for as long as he held her.

'Ready for the crowds?' he asked. 'The reception committee and the Press are waiting for you in the clubhouse.'

'All I really want is a hot shower and a comfortable bed,' Lara replied.

'Later, I promise,' Dexter said.

'Hang on, I've forgotten something.' Lara dived back down below, emerging seconds later with Nero and Fred Bear clutched tightly to her.

'Can't leave them behind,' she said. 'They'd miss me.'

It took some time to make any progress towards the clubhouse, as everyone they passed wanted to congratulate Lara.

Cassie watched proudly as 'Little Lara', as everybody now seemed determined to call her, made her second place acceptance speech.

It was only as Nigel made his speech and laughingly warned her, 'I'll be chasing you even harder in the next leg, Little Lara,' that Cassie remembered this wasn't the end.

Lara still had over twenty thousand miles to sail and a lot of those miles would be in the inhospitable and dangerous Southern Ocean.

8

A Farewell Supper

Lara glanced at Cassie as she packed. 'It's been a great four days. I'm so glad you came, Mum.'

'Thank you for making it possible,' Cassie replied. She looked affectionately at her daughter.

'It didn't bring back too many sad memories?' Lara asked quietly.

Cassie shook her head.

'It's completely different from the days when your dad was competing. There's much more razzmatazz — more fun altogether. Although I don't suppose the actual sailing has changed much. It's still pretty tough out there, isn't it?'

'I love the challenge,' Lara replied. 'And at least I didn't disgrace myself on Leg One. Even Tom admitted second place was a result!'

'The next two legs are a different prospect, though, aren't they? The Southern Ocean followed by Cape Horn,' Cassie said quietly.

'Mum, it will be fine,' Lara reassured her.

'Now, are you going to wear your new dress this evening?' she said, changing the subject.

'You don't think it's a bit over the top?' Cassie fingered the soft chiffon material of the dress she'd fallen for in an upmarket designer store on the waterfront.

'Of course not,' Lara said. 'It really suits you.'

Cassie glanced at her watch.

'What time is Dexter picking us up?' she asked.

'In about half an hour. While you finish packing I'll grab a shower.' Lara vanished into the bathroom.

Dexter was waiting for them in the hotel foyer when they went downstairs, ready to drive them out to Becky and

Trev's house in the suburbs.

Becky had insisted on organising a farewell supper for Cassie.

'It's the least I can do now we've met up again. Besides, I want you to see my home.'

Situated on the edge of a cliff overlooking the Atlantic Ocean, the house had spectacular views and was clearly a much-loved home.

Trev had done well with his yachting and chartering business, Cassie thought.

Inevitably, the conversation was very yacht orientated and Cassie found herself laughing as Trev told the other guests about events from their past.

She even found herself recalling a couple of incidents Trev had forgotten, involving herself and Miles — happy memories she hadn't thought about in years.

Looking at her old friends, Cassie felt a twinge of sadness for the lost years. She'd been silly to cut herself off from those people who'd meant so much to her.

It was Lara who brought her back into the conversation.

'Has Mum told you her plans for changing her life now that Tom's married and I'm off sailing?' she asked Becky. 'It's her way of beating the empty-nest syndrome.'

Becky glanced at Cassie. Like Lara, she knew it was more than empty-nest syndrome Cassie was attempting to fight. They'd always been able to confide in each other. The years apart hadn't changed that.

'She's mentioned moving into a small cottage, doing her own thing,' Becky said. 'I think it's an excellent idea.'

'Actually,' Trev interrupted, 'I've got an even better one.' He turned to Cassie.

'Why don't you come and live here?'

'Trev, you're brilliant!' Becky exclaimed. 'Why didn't I think of that? Cassie, why not? You say it's time to do something different with your life, lay all those ghosts. Well, do it here. Come and live with us. We've plenty of room. Come for six months and see what happens.'

'There you go, Mum. What an opportunity!' Lara was full of enthusiasm for the plan, but Cassie was rendered completely speechless!

Thinking Ahead

Mai was driving Tom back from the hospital, where he'd had the heavy plaster casts taken off his legs and replaced with less cumbersome splints.

'I know it's early days yet, but I've been thinking about godparents for the baby,' she said.

'Lara for one of the godmothers,' Tom replied.

'We'll have to choose names, too. Or should we wait and see what the baby looks like first? I have to admit I like old-fashioned names rather than trendy modern ones.'

'Good,' Mai agreed. 'I've been favouring Alice for a girl and Samuel for a boy.'

'Your old room can be the nursery. We'll paint it pale yellow and light blue,' Mai continued enthusiastically. 'I've seen some lovely wallpaper.'

'We're taking Mum up on her offer, then?' Tom asked quietly.

'You have doubts?'

'I just don't want Mum feeling she's being pushed out of her own home.'

'According to Anna, this is something she really wants to do.'

Mai drove into the boatyard and parked.

'Mum's due back in a couple of days. Before then we must all get together and make plans for her birthday next month. She's fifty, so we'll have to organise something special,' Tom said.

Break-in

Just then, Anna appeared to give Mai a hand helping Tom out of the car and on to crutches for the first time. She seemed distracted.

'Is something the matter, Anna?' Mai asked.

Anna sighed.

'River View has been broken into. James says it looks as though someone was planning to squat there. Nothing seems to be missing and they've found a sleeping bag upstairs. Bill's there now, repairing the window and trying to make the place more secure.'

'When did it happen?' Tom asked.

'James noticed the broken window this morning as he was doing one of his regular river patrols. He suggested we tighten security here and in the boatyard. A couple of the boats down river have had outboard motors taken,' Anna said.

'Does James have any idea who's responsible?' Tom asked.

Anna shook her head.

'Apparently there have been a few strangers around recently, including the shifty boy we saw on the river path, but there's nothing to link them to anything.

'I'm heading off to the cottage to do a spot of clearing up before Cassie gets home. Do you have time to join me, Mai?'

'Of course,' Mai agreed.

'You'd better take Solo with you,' Tom said. 'And can you ask Gramps if he has any ideas for Mum's party?'

*　*　*

Cassie shivered as the cold British air hit her the moment she stepped out on to the airport concourse. The all-too-familiar overcast sky after the blue of South Africa was an instant reminder of the beautiful weather she'd left Lara enjoying in the countdown to the next leg of the race.

She was about to drag her suitcase along to the taxi rank when she heard her name being called.

'Cassie, wait!'

Turning, she was surprised to see Doug striding towards her.

'I'm sorry I'm late. I wanted to be

here in the arrivals lounge to meet you, but I was held up.

'Here, let me carry that.' Doug took the suitcase from her.

'Did you have a good flight?'

Cassie nodded.

'Yes, thanks. What are you doing here anyway?' she asked.

'I was on my way back from Scotland and thought you might like some company for the last part of your journey home.' Doug smiled at her.

Doug's car, a seriously upmarket model with a luxurious leather interior, was soon eating up the motorway miles. Cassie began to relax.

'Tell me about your holiday,' Doug said. 'Did you take the cable car to the top of Table Mountain? Visit Robben Island? Go whale watching?'

'Yes, yes and no. It was the wrong season for whales. But there was so much else to do and see, the days went by far too quickly. Lara and I had a wonderful time.

'And I had a lovely surprise, too. I

met up with some old friends.' Cassie told Doug about Becky and Trev.

A few miles further on, Doug pulled off the motorway for petrol.

'I thought we'd stop for lunch, too. There's a good restaurant nearby where I usually call in on my way down. You don't have to be back by any particular time, do you?'

Cassie shook her head.

At the restaurant, Cassie popped into the cloakroom to freshen up. When she made her way back to the table, she found Vanessa had joined Doug.

'Hi. I took a chance Dad would be here. I know it's a favourite watering hole on his drive south. There are a couple of things I need to discuss with him. I didn't expect to see you.'

'I didn't expect him to meet me at the airport, either,' Cassie said lightly.

Had she imagined it, or was there a definite edge to Vanessa's voice?

'You could have called me on the mobile if things were that urgent,' Doug pointed out brusquely.

'I know, Dad,' Vanessa said, 'but I wanted to see you.' She threaded her arm through her father's, smiling up at him.

'You've been in Scotland for ages.'

They ate their meal, which was as delicious as Doug had promised it would be, and Cassie sat and listened as Vanessa firmly kept the conversation business orientated, despite Doug's attempts to include Cassie in a more general way.

Doug was clearly irritated.

'Right, that's enough business talk, Vanessa,' he said before the desserts arrived. 'Poor Cassie must be wondering where our manners are.'

'Oh, Cassie, I'm sorry,' Vanessa cooed. 'Do tell us about your holiday. Dad and I love Cape Town, don't we? Do you remember the time . . . ' She launched into a rambling reminiscence of a long-ago holiday incident.

Cassie, finding herself once again excluded from the conversation between daughter and father, began to wish for the meal to be over. Why was Vanessa being so rude? And why was Doug letting her get away with it?

'Interference'

Part of the answer came when Doug excused himself and went to pay the bill at the bar.

'Daddy has never looked at another woman since Mummy left, so don't get any ideas about bagging a rich husband,' Vanessa said aggressively.

Cassie was completely taken aback. Her first instinct was to tell this disagreeable young woman to mind her own business in no uncertain terms. However, she managed to keep her temper under control, and when she spoke, her voice was calm.

'Vanessa, your father and I met only recently and he's been very kind to me and my family. I've been on my own for twenty years and I assure you I'm not desperate for a husband, rich or otherwise. The idea that Doug regards me as anything other than a friend is ludicrous.' Cassie took a breath.

'I will just say this, however. Don't you think your father is entitled to choose his own friends, without your interference? Maybe after all the years on his own, he's feeling lonely — especially now you and your sister live your own lives.' She paused.

'I'll leave you to say goodbye to your father. Perhaps you'd be kind enough to tell him I'll see him by the car. Goodbye, Vanessa.' Cassie turned away.

By the time Doug joined her ten minutes later, Cassie had recovered her composure.

'Thank you for lunch.' She greeted him with a smile.

Doug put the key into the ignition, but instead of starting the car, he sat back, hands gripping the steering wheel.

'Cassie, I can only apologise for Vanessa. I had no idea she would waylay me here, or that she would behave as she did. I'd hoped she'd outgrown the antagonism she's always shown towards any of my female friends.

'The last thing I want is for her to frighten you away.'

'Doug, it's all right,' Cassie said, touching his arm. 'I'll survive. And we can still be friends. The only thing that bothers me is, why didn't you stand up to her in the restaurant?'

Doug looked at her.

'If it had happened somewhere private I would have. But you have no idea of the scene Vanessa can cause if she wants to. I had no intention of subjecting you to that in public.'

He started the engine and slowly reversed the car out of its parking space.

'I suppose, when their mother left, I made the classic mistake of over-compensating with the girls. Caroline coped really well but Vanessa has always had a possessive streak and I did nothing to curb it. I guess I was out of my depth. I should have done things differently.'

'We can only do our best in the circumstances at the time. Looking back, wanting to change things, is a futile exercise.' Cassie sighed.

'I can promise you one thing, Cassie — the next time we have a meal together, it will be just the two of us. Now, let's get you home. It's been a long day for you.'

Cassie, happy to sit watching the countryside flash by, let her thoughts drift. She'd spent most of the flight considering Becky and Trev's tempting offer. Now, though, as the car crossed the familiar Somerset-Devonshire border, a comfortable feeling came over her.

She was nearly home. This was where she belonged and where she'd build the new life she intended to forge for herself.

Going to South Africa to live was a tempting idea, but not one she intended to put into practice. She wanted to stay in Devon.

'An Isolated Incident'

A week later, Cassie was regarding her handiwork in the sitting-room at River View. It had taken two days of intensive labour to transform the place. She'd cleaned and scrubbed the kitchen and bathroom and had painted the sitting-room a delicate shade of primrose yellow. The new carpet was due tomorrow.

She jumped as Solo barked and a loud knock on the door interrupted her thoughts.

'It's only me,' Anna called. 'I wondered if you had the time and energy for a walk. Hey, this place looks great.'

'I can't believe I'm moving in here before you get the keys to Glebe House,' Cassie said. 'Don't forget, if you want a hand cleaning and painting. I'm your woman.'

'I'll hold you to that,' Anna said.

'Cassie, are you sure you're OK about living here on your own — especially after the break-in?'

'I don't think I'd be happy without Solo,' Cassie said slowly. 'But I've got her and the telephone. Also, it's the first break-in in all the years Dad's owned the place, so I think it was just an isolated incident — some kid running away from home, or something.'

She picked up Solo's lead and they headed off.

'Have you seen James since you've been back?' Anna asked.

Cassie shook her head.

'I've spoken to him on the phone, but things have been so hectic I haven't had a moment to spare.'

Solo bounded ahead of them down the river path, leaving Cassie and Anna to follow. One of the large tourist boats was making its way downriver, loudspeaker booming out information.

As the boat drew level with Holdsworth Boatyard and Marina, the loudspeaker crackled into life again.

'Here on the right is the childhood home of Lara Lewis, the yachtswoman. It was on this river that Lara learned to sail. Now she's the youngest skipper taking part in a gruelling solo race around the world.'

Cassie looked at Anna in amazement before bursting into laughter.

'I don't believe it. Lara's a local tourist attraction! I can't wait to tell her.'

'Just You And Me'

The sun was setting, throwing Table Mountain into silhouette against the evening sky as Lara made her way towards the yacht club. All around, the lights of the city were beginning to twinkle.

Smiling to herself, Lara remembered the evening Dexter had taken her and Cassie on a whirlwind tour of the city's nightlife. It was two o'clock in the morning before he'd led them back to the hotel, totally exhausted.

It was Dexter who'd taken them around during the daytime, too, showing them the sights. A visit out to

Robben Island, a drive along the Stellenbosch Wine Route and, of course, the cable car up Table Mountain.

He'd spent as much time as he could with them during Cassie's visit. Since she'd left, Dexter had returned to his mountain of paperwork and Lara had seen little of him.

The days had passed in a blur of chores as Lara and the shore crew worked all hours, preparing *Clotted Cream* for the next stage of the race. Tonight, though, just a day away from the start, she was meeting Dexter for a final stroll around Cape Town.

'Just you and me, Lara,' he'd said. 'No shore team, no other skippers.'

Dexter was waiting for her as promised outside the yacht club.

'I thought we'd just wander and listen to some jazz down on the waterfront,' he said, taking her hand.

'Have you talked to Tom yet about your route?'

'He e-mailed this morning with his

recommendations. You've sailed this route before, too, haven't you?'

Dexter nodded.

'I always think of this section as offering some seriously good sailing, although it is dangerous, no doubt about it. I was fortunate enough to have reasonable weather when I did it.' He looked at Lara.

'If you're really lucky you'll get to see the Southern Lights. It's an incredible experience.'

Further along the quay they found a table at one of the many cafés and Dexter ordered coffee.

'Are you flying straight to New Zealand from here or do you get time off to go home while we battle our way through the Southern Ocean?' Lara asked.

'I have to stay in touch in case there are any emergencies, but in theory I've got two weeks to call my own. I'm going back to the UK to see my family. I'm also trying to sell my apartment in New York so I guess

I should try to get over there, too.'

'Are you buying somewhere else in America?'

Dexter shrugged.

'I don't know. My contract with the race organisers finishes after this race. I have to decide whether to renew it and stay in America, or join my dad in the family farm.'

'I thought you loved being involved with boats?'

'I do, but the problem is I don't get to do much sailing these days. If I take a regular land-based job. I could at least do some pleasure sailing. What about you? Do you have any plans for when the race is over?'

'Not really. Hopefully I'll finish in a good position and somebody will offer me a boat of my own.' She shrugged.

'If not, I'll probably do some more crewing and help Tom and Mai build up the sailing school. I know Mum favours that option.' She smiled.

'Are you still in touch with Sebastian?' Dexter asked unexpectedly.

'He phoned me yesterday, actually. Believe it or not, he's still trying to persuade me to give up the race!'

She took a breath.

'I'll e-mail him again once I'm at sea and try to get him to accept the fact that my answer to everything he's asked has to be no.'

She remembered the ring in the drawer at home.

'But I guess he won't admit it's all over between us until I tell him face to face,' she added.

There was silence for a moment before Dexter stood up and held out his hand.

'Come on, let's walk back to *Clotted Cream*.'

Sitting out on deck an hour later, Dexter's arm casually around her shoulders, Lara experienced a moment of pure happiness sweep through her. This was an evening she'd remember and relive many times as she made her way across the Southern Ocean.

She turned towards him as Dexter

gently pulled her closer.

'I'll be waiting for you in New Zealand, Little Lara,' he whispered, before kissing her and holding her tight.

'Sail safe.'

9

A Good Start

Cassie finally moved into River View Cottage the day Lara set sail from Cape Town for New Zealand.

Earlier, she'd been in the kitchen at Boatyard House with Mai and Tom, avidly watching the internet link-up with its minute-by-minute update of the race.

To everyone's delight, Lara crossed the start line in second place, sandwiched between Colin on *World Wanderer* in the lead and Nigel on *Flight Of The Seagull* in third place. The first three in from the previous leg were the first three out across the line.

Tom had sent an e-mail.

Congratulations on your excellent start, Lara. Good luck for the next seven thousand miles. Speak to you later. Love from everybody.

Now, as Cassie emptied the last of the boxes and put her books and photographs on the newly built shelves in the sitting-room at the cottage, she firmly pushed worrying thoughts about Lara out of her mind. There was, after all, very little she could do if anything were to go wrong — which it wouldn't.

Going through to the tiny kitchen, Cassie made herself a cup of coffee and checked the time. Anna had been in Wales for a few days, organising the removal of some of her things.

Cassie had promised to collect her from the station. If she wasn't going to be late she'd better get a move on.

⋆   ⋆   ⋆

'How was it?' she asked as she helped Anna put her suitcases in the car boot.

'Rained non-stop as usual.' Anna smiled. 'It was great to see everybody, though. David is bringing the last of my stuff down next week. I've warned him he'll be sleeping on the floor — there isn't a bed in the spare room yet.'

'There's always my old room at Tom and Mai's,' Cassie said. 'Solo and I finally moved into River View Cottage today.'

'Congratulations. Are you fed up with decorating or can you face giving me a hand at Glebe House?'

'Mornings are out this week, I'm afraid. There's a party of three on the barge who want sailing lessons. But I can definitely offer my services a couple of afternoons. When are you planning to move in?'

'Probably the day the furniture arrives. I hoped to stay on at Boatyard House for a few more days — if it's OK with Tom and Mai.'

'I can't see it being a problem,' Cassie said.

Declining the offer of coffee when she dropped Anna at the house, Cassie decided to leave her car in the garage at the yard and walk back to River View Cottage.

It felt strange, closing the kitchen door behind her and leaving everyone chatting in what she still thought of as her kitchen, to go back to the empty cottage. Fleetingly, Cassie wondered if she'd done the right thing.

Was she going to be lonely, living on her own? At least this evening it wouldn't be a problem. She had a guest for supper.

A Grateful Hug

Music playing in the background, scented candles to keep the twilight midges at bay, a table set for two on the small patio, supper sizzling in the oven, wine opened to breathe and Cassie was ready.

She spotted the launch coming upriver and she and Solo walked down to the landing stage to meet her guest.

'I hope it's still warm enough to eat outside,' she said. 'But if you're cold we can carry the table indoors.'

'Outside is fine,' James said, brushing her cheek with his lips.

'Do I get a guided tour before we eat?'

'It won't take long.' Cassie laughed. 'What you see is all there is.

'Oh, before I forget, I have a present for you from South Africa. I'm sorry it's a bit late.'

'You've been busy getting this place ready and I've . . . well, I've had other things on my mind, too,' James said.

As Cassie had hoped, James loved the original watercolour painting of an old J class yacht sailing off the South African coast.

'I thought it would go well with the rest of your collection.'

'Pride of place for this. Thank you so much, Cassie.' James gave her a grateful hug.

They'd almost finished supper when Cassie picked up on what James had said earlier.

'What's been on your mind these past few weeks, then?' she asked.

'The powers that be are trying to rearrange the management of all the harbours along this part of the coast. Their aim is to cut expenses — and reduce manpower.' James looked at Cassie.

'Their latest proposal is to combine my job with that of Harbour Master for the Old Port.'

'But the Old Port is fifteen miles down the coast. You can't be in two places at once. And think of the waste of time commuting between the two. It's just silly.'

'I know. You know. But the committee is determined. The question now is, which Harbour Master's job is going to disappear?'

Cassie looked at him as he abstractedly rearranged the salt and pepper pots on the table.

'Perhaps, more to the point is, do I want the job even if they offer it to me?' James glanced up at her.

'I've had enough stress with just one harbour to look after. If they suggest redundancy, I think I'm going to take it.'

'Do you have any idea what you'd do afterwards?'

James shook his head.

'Depending on the pay-out, perhaps I could look around for some part-time work.'

Look around? Cassie was surprised at how desolate she felt at the thought of her dear friend moving out of her life. But his next words allayed her fears.

'All I really know is that I want to stay in the area, even if money does become a bit tight.' He smiled at Cassie.

'I'll certainly be free to do more sailing, which will be a bonus. Incidentally, are you free to crew for me in a race this Saturday? It's the course out in the bay towards the Skerries.'

'As long as we're back by about six o'clock. It's my birthday next week and I gather Tom and Dad are organising a dinner at the Seafarer's for me on Saturday evening. Can you come?'

'I wouldn't miss it. In fact, I'll be your chauffeur for the evening.'

'Thanks.' Cassie smiled.

'Is Saturday your actual birthday?'

'No, it's on Wednesday. But partying is always better at the weekend. Nobody has to get up for work the next day.'

Cassie shivered suddenly.

'Come on, let's take our coffee indoors. I'm sure you're feeling cold by now. I know I am.'

She stood up and led the way into the sitting-room.

Lara's Journal

Sunday 20th.
Well, at least I made a good start again. It was a shame I couldn't get across the line in front of World Wanderer — but I've got the next seven thousand miles to catch Colin up and pass him!

I've settled back into my daily routine and I've even e-mailed my latest piece to the newspaper a day early. They've asked if I'd be prepared to visit a few schools during the stopover in Brazil and give talks to the children.

I'll have to think about that. I've got to reach New Zealand first and then make my way around Cape Horn. Everybody says the leg from New Zealand to Brazil is the toughest of the race.

Six days after rounding Cape Point and the fleet is well spread out. I can't even see another sail in the distance and I'm getting used to being alone again.

The sailing, as Dexter predicted it could be, has been fantastic, but I'm beginning to worry about icebergs.

Having Mum around in Cape Town was great. I hope she enjoyed it as much as I did. It's a pity she won't be in the other ports.

Dexter has been either e-mailing or telephoning me every day. He's still in the UK with his family and it sounds as *if he's coming round to the idea of joining his father on the family farm.*

I can see Dexter as a farmer. He'd enjoy the life, I'm sure.

According to HQ we're in for some stormy weather. I'm as well prepared as I can be. The guys back in Cape Town did a brilliant job on Clotted Cream, getting her ready for this leg. I've battened everything down that I can and I'm keeping my fingers crossed that the winds don't blow too strong.

Two e-mails just came in. One was from Sebastian telling me his exercise is over and he's back in the UK. He hopes I'm OK and he's looking forward to seeing me when the race is over to sort things out. Mmm. I wish I could say the same.

I hate the thought of hurting him, but since I've been at sea I've really had time to think and I know I don't want to spend the rest of my life with Sebastian. Somehow, I have to tell him and make the break.

The other e-mail was from Dexter,

adding his personal warning about gale force winds.

A week later.

I've just lived through the most amazing week of my life. The storm was unbelievably violent. For three days Clotted Cream took a tremendous pasting. We were so lucky that nothing major broke.

I've managed to clear up some of the mess in the cabin, but my main concern is the sails. As soon as the winds drop a bit, I'll get the sewing stuff out and have a major maintenance session on them.

Yesterday the sun forced its way through the grey clouds and the change in the sea colour was incredible.

And last night the Southern Lights were all around me — flashes of green and yellow exploding in the sky. It was an incredible sight that I wanted to share with someone, so I rang Dexter on the satellite phone. I think I got him out of bed — I'd completely forgotten the time difference.

He was incredibly sweet about it and chatted for ages. He flies out to New Zealand tomorrow to start organising things for us all there.

With luck, fourteen days should see me sailing into Tauranga. World Wanderer is twenty-two hours ahead of me so I've got some hard sailing ahead if I want to catch Colin.

Mounting Horror

Cassie woke up on the morning of her birthday to hear the rain still drumming on to the cottage patio. It had been pouring non-stop now for almost a week.

Glancing out of the window, she could see that the river had risen several inches overnight. The landing stage was submerged and, with mounting horror, she realised the water was now over the bottom two steps of the flight leading up to the cottage.

Her father had sent up some

sandbags and she'd dutifully placed them around the front door of the cottage, never believing it was necessary. This morning, with the water only a foot away, it looked as if they might be needed after all.

She picked up the phone.

'Tom, is everything all right down there? The river seems to have burst its banks here.'

'It's very swollen and running a lot faster than normal, but so far we're OK,' Tom said. 'I think you should make your way down here. Shall I get Gramps to come up in the launch for you?'

'No, I reckon Solo and I can come round the back way. I'll just pile things on top of each other first and hope for the best. I'll see you within the next hour.'

'OK. And, Mum, happy birthday.'

In the kitchen Cassie unplugged the fridge and the oven and pulled the mat up in front of the back door. In the sitting-room she piled as many of her electrical things as she could on the table.

Finally she unplugged the phone and put that on top.

'Come on, Solo, let's make for dry ground.' She headed out, locking the door behind her.

The water was still a foot away from the top step and Cassie could only hope that it would stop raining soon.

By the time she made it into the kitchen at Boatyard House, she was exhausted and soaked through. Gratefully she cradled the mug of hot coffee that Mai handed her.

'Do you think it's ever going to stop raining?' she said.

'According to the Met, it should ease off this afternoon, but they're forecasting more for the weekend,' Tom replied.

'How are the people out on the barge?' Cassie asked.

'Quite safe. Gramps has been out to check the mooring and it's holding fast in the swell. He's told them not to attempt to leave the barge until the tide turns.

'He's offered to ferry them to and

from shore in the launch.'

Mai put some cards and packages on the table.

'Happy birthday, Cassie,' she said. 'I hope you're planning to spend the day here.'

'Thank you, Mai. I'm supposed to be lunching with Doug on *Megabyte* and this evening I'm having supper with Anna. Other than that, I'd love to spend the day here.'

'Birthday lunch with Doug? Is there something you should tell us, Mum?' Tom teased.

'Certainly not.' Cassie laughed. 'Today just happens to be the only one Doug has free from business commitments. I don't think he even knows it's my birthday.'

She could feel the colour rising in her cheeks and hoped Tom would change the subject.

She liked Doug and enjoyed his company, but she didn't want anybody reading things into their relationship that simply weren't there.

★ ★ ★

Doug, however, did know it was her birthday, as was evident by the bottle of champagne in the ice bucket and the gift-wrapped package waiting for her in *Megabyte's* dining saloon.

'Oh, Doug. I didn't think you knew,' Cassie exclaimed.

'Happy birthday and many more of them,' Doug said.

He poured her a glass of champagne.

The gold bracelet with its inlaid amber stones was exquisite.

'I wanted to give you something to remember such a momentous occasion,' Doug said quietly, taking her hand in his. 'And to mark what I hope is the beginning of more than friendship between us.'

His words hung in the air as he looked at her, waiting for her reaction.

Cassie took a deep breath and withdrew her hand.

'The bracelet's beautiful, Doug, but I can't accept it. It's far too early in our friendship for you to be buying me such an expensive birthday present.

'What happens if our friendship doesn't develop into anything more? I'd feel guilty every time I wore the bracelet and you'd regret having spent such a lot of money on someone who didn't return your feelings.'

It was several seconds before Doug spoke.

'Cassie, I'm sorry, I didn't mean to embarrass you. I merely wanted to give you a nice present.

'It's been a long time since I've met a woman I like as much as you. I'm clearly out of practice with the social niceties and have jumped in too quickly.' He paused.

'Please accept the bracelet as a special birthday present from a new friend with no other motive. Next time, I'll ask your permission before I buy you anything.' This last was said with such a twinkle in his eyes that Cassie laughed in spite of herself.

'It's been a long time for me, too,

since anybody wanted to buy me expensive presents and it is beautiful,' she confessed. 'As a special birthday present, then. Thank you very much.' Shyly, she stood on her tiptoes and kissed his cheek.

Doug sighed with relief.

'Good. Now that's sorted, let's have lunch.'

'Take Care'

The rain had eased slightly by the time Cassie drove into town to have supper with Anna. She'd almost cancelled after James's phone call but Tom and Mai persuaded her to go.

James had been upriver to check on the various moorings and had rung to say that, although the water was still lapping around the cottage steps, it didn't appear to be getting any higher.

'Have you locked the cottage up securely?' he asked just before ringing off.

'Yes, of course, Why?'

'Somebody seems to have taken advantage of the bad weather and broken into several boats. I've got another patrol tonight so I'll check on the cottage, just in case.'

'Thanks. James?'

'Yes?'

'You will take care, won't you? No heroics?'

There was a chuckle at the end of the line before James replied.

'I promise, no heroics. Enjoy your supper with Anna and I'll see you on Saturday morning.'

Now, as she and Anna tucked into their favourite lasagne at the wine bar in town, Cassie told Anna about her day — and the present from Doug.

'It's a lovely bracelet. It obviously cost a fortune and although I know he can afford it, I still can't help feeling it's a bit over the top for someone you don't know that well.'

'Like he said, he's hoping you will get to know each other better.'

'But I feel as if he's bribing me to like him,' Cassie admitted. 'Does that sound stupid? And I feel guilty now because he's not invited to my birthday dinner on Saturday — even though he did say he was away again at the weekend.

'Incidentally, do you know who exactly is coming? Tom and Dad haven't said. And the Seafarer's is a bit on the expensive side for too many people.'

'I shouldn't worry,' Anna said. 'I think your dad is more than willing to push the boat out for you. Just enjoy it.'

'You Look Beautiful'

By Saturday the rain had eased and the fears of flooding had receded. Cassie and James, making their way out to the Skerries, found there was a strong enough wind to make for exciting sailing.

Although they finished the race in ninth place, they both agreed it had been a good day.

'I'll be back to pick you up at eight o'clock,' James promised. 'Cottage or Boatyard House?'

'Boatyard House, please. It's still very muddy at the cottage.'

Tom and Mai had already left by the time James arrived.

Cassie was wearing the dress she'd bought in Cape Town, which drew an appreciative whistle from James.

'You look beautiful, Cassie. These are for you. If you don't like them, please say so. We can take them back and you can choose something else.'

He watched anxiously as Cassie unwrapped her present to reveal a pair of aquamarine earrings.

'James, they're lovely. I'm going to wear them tonight. They're a perfect match for my dress.' Cassie fixed them into her ears, banishing a fleeting pang of guilt about the gold and amber bracelet she'd left lying upstairs in its box.

Turning to give James a thank-you

kiss, she found herself enveloped unexpectedly in a tight hug.

'Happy birthday, Cassie,' James whispered before he kissed her.

Seconds later he released her.

'Let's party,' he said, taking her hand.

'Surprise!'

At the Country Club he held her hand again as they made their way through the foyer.

At the foot of the stairs she automatically turned for the restaurant.

'No, this way, Cassie.' James headed towards the function room.

Cassie pointed at the sign.

'It's closed for a special . . . ' Her voice trailed away as James opened the door and she was greeted by fifty people all shouting 'Surprise!' at the tops of their voices.

Turning to James, she laughed.

'You could have warned me,' she said, before walking into the room to be surrounded by her family and friends.

She was dancing an energetic Charleston with James later in the evening, when she saw Tom answer his mobile phone and glance across at her. His expression was serious and she was already moving towards him as he beckoned her over.

'Mum, it's Lara.' He handed the phone to her.

'Hi, Mum. Sorry to interrupt the party. I hope you're having fun.'

'Yes, thanks. Are you all right?'

'I have to tell you something before you hear it on the news.'

Cassie waited, her heart in her mouth.

'One of the other skippers has had an accident. As I'm the nearest boat I've been asked to alter course and give assistance. Dexter will ring you later and fill you in on all the details. I just wanted to tell you not to worry.'

10

'Fire!'

Cassie put the phone down and turned to Tom. 'Lara said Dexter will ring with more details. I suppose she means in the morning.' Cassie's lips quivered.

'Try not to worry, Mum.' Tom's tone was reassuring. 'It's not Lara who's in trouble, remember.'

In the background Cassie heard the band start up again.

'James is waiting for another dance,' Tom pointed out.

'Oh, I couldn't,' Cassie began.

'Yes, you can,' James interrupted and led her back on to the floor. 'It's still your birthday party, so try to enjoy the rest of it.'

And Cassie found herself doing just that. Maybe the extra glass of champagne that James gave her had something to do with it, but she did manage to put her worries about Lara to the back of her mind for the rest of the evening.

It was after midnight before the last of her friends said goodnight.

James drove her home.

'They say fifty is the new forty, these days.' He laughed. 'So how does it feel to be forty?'

Cassie smothered a yawn.

'I'm looking forward to my bed tonight more than I did after my real fortieth! I definitely haven't got the stamina for late nights any more.'

'I know what you mean,' James agreed. 'I'm good on early mornings, though.'

'It's a bit misty tonight, isn't it?' Cassie peered out of the window.

'Actually, I think it looks more like smoke. There's probably a chimney fire somewhere,' James answered.

'Now, are you spending the night at Boatyard House or am I driving you back to the cottage?' he asked as they approached the crossroads.

'Boatyard House, please. I haven't set the cottage to rights yet since the river burst its banks. Besides, I left Solo at the house.'

Just then, James pulled over to the verge and stopped. Cassie looked at him in surprise.

'Is something the matter? Have we broken down?' she asked.

'No. There's a flashing blue light behind.'

They both watched the police car drive past with a grateful toot of its horn.

Cassie looked at James in dismay.

'Apart from the Henshawes' place, this road only goes to the boatyard before it loops back up to the main road!'

Without a word James began to follow the police car as it made its way quickly down to the boatyard.

As they drove the atmosphere outside became steadily thicker and there was a definite smell of pungent smoke. Cassie took a deep breath.

'James, I think Boatyard House is on fire.'

'I can't see any flames,' he answered shortly, but as they drove into the yard it became evident that there had been flames — lots of them. Not in the house itself, but in the workshops.

Bill and Rufus were talking to the police as the firemen began to tidy up their equipment.

'Where's Solo? What's happened?' Cassie asked anxiously.

'She's in the house and she's fine,' Bill assured her. 'Everything is under control.'

'By the look of the front door somebody tried to break into the house and your dog went potty. The front door is scratched to bits inside,' one of the policemen said.

'I'm afraid they had better luck with the workshops. They got away with a lot of tools before setting fire to the place.'

'Oh, Dad, I'm so sorry. If it hadn't been for my birthday party, someone would have been here and it wouldn't have happened.'

'That's silly talk, Cassie. I reckon they were just biding their time.'

'Any idea yet who's responsible?' Cassie asked the policeman.

He shook his head.

'It's too soon to say. All we know so far is they came and left by boat. There were two or three of them, judging by the number of new muddy footprints we've found. We'll need to get forensics out here first thing in the morning. The brigade will be doing their own tests, too.' He nodded in the direction of the firemen.

'I'm afraid I have to ask you not to touch anything before they've been.'

'I reckon we all want our beds anyway,' Bill said. 'We're too tired to start clearing up now.'

'By the way, who called the fire brigade?' Cassie asked.

'The couple on the barge. They used their mobile,' a fireman said.

One of the policemen glanced at James.

'Could I have an official word, Captain White, before we go?'

'Of course.' James nodded.

Bill and Rufus gave Cassie a hand taking her presents into the house whilst James talked to the policeman. Finally, Cassie touched James on the arm.

'I'm sorry to interrupt, James, but I'm off to bed. I just wanted to say goodnight — and thank you.'

'Goodnight, Cassie. I'll ring you tomorrow.'

As she went indoors Cassie heard the policeman speak quietly to James.

'If it could be a joint operation I feel we'd have a better chance of catching them.'

Lara's Journal

Monday 14th.

It's thirty-six hours now since I altered course and effectively took myself out of the race for this leg. I can't help feeling disappointed, but I know if I'd run into trouble, one of the guys would have done the same for me.

The weather isn't too bad — no storms are forecast in the immediate future, anyway.

I've been reading up on my first aid in case Jean-Paul is in a worse state than he says.

We've been e-mailing each other and I've spoken to him on the phone, so he knows I should be with him in the next twelve hours.

The plan is for me to sail alongside and get him on board Clotted Cream. Then we wait for an Australian frigate that's been asked to divert and assist.

They'll take Jean-Paul on board and I'll sail back to my last official position and head for New Zealand again.

I've re-angled the video camera on the mast so I should have a record of what happens when I reach Jean-Paul. We're so far from land I know there won't be TV crews around to film any drama.

Dexter has warned me, though, that they'll be waiting for me in their droves when I finally get to New Zealand.

I'm going to have a bowl of pasta and a quick sleep before I have a mammoth session on the satellite phone. I know Mum and Tom will be anxious for news and Dexter always rings to wish me goodnight.

'I Need To Talk To You'

It was a question of all hands to the mop and broom in the boatyard once the forensic teams had given them the all clear and the insurance assessor had been.

As Cassie threw some charred wood into the rubbish skip Bill had organised, the telephone rang.

It was Dexter.

'What's happening?' Cassie asked anxiously.

'Lara's due to reach Jean-Paul in a few hours and everything is looking good. She was fine when I spoke to her this morning. She's a bit apprehensive as to what she's going to find, but Jean-Paul says the yacht is in a worse state than he is.'

Although Dexter spoke confidently there was a certain edge to his voice and Cassie knew he, too, would be worried about Lara. She'd noticed how close they were becoming when she'd flown out to South Africa for the end of the first leg of the race.

'She's going to ring you later.'

'Thanks, Dexter. I'll speak to you again soon.'

As Cassie put the phone down Tom came struggling into the boatyard on his crutches.

'Mum, I need to talk to you,' he announced.

Cassie threw another piece of charred wood in the direction of the rubbish skip and waited.

'You know I'm due to have these things off soon?' He tapped the plaster on his legs.

Cassie nodded.

'The thing is, I'd like to take Mai away afterwards, just for a few days.'

'Good idea,' Cassie said.

'But there are a couple of problems,' Tom went on. 'One is the barge. We have bookings so it would mean a lot of extra work for you. And you're already doing so much.'

'Don't worry about me,' Cassie said quickly. 'Besides, Anna will come and give me a hand. She likes being here. Next problem?'

'Lara's operational room. Because of this rescue and the fact that Race HQ are currently in constant contact with her, it doesn't have to be manned twenty-four hours a day. But you would need to update the computer a couple of times a day.'

'I'm sure I can manage that if you show me how before you leave. Where are you going?'

'Not Really My Scene'

'I thought we might go up to London — see a show, do some shopping, be tourists for a day or two.

'I think Mai misses city life occasionally.'

'It sounds fun. Why don't you see how you manage when the plaster comes off and then decide on a date?

'I'm here and happy to handle things.'

'Thanks, Mum.'

'Where's Mai now?'

'She's gone out to the barge with a large box of chocolates and a bottle of wine to say thank you for raising the alarm.' Tom glanced around.

'Bad as it is, it could have been a lot worse. Do the police reckon they'll catch whoever did it?'

'It's too soon to say.'

Just then the phone rang again.

'I'll see you later. Mum.' Tom manoeuvred his way out of the shed.

'Cassie, I've just heard about the fire.'

Doug's voice made Cassie jump. She'd been expecting James.

'Is there anything I can do? I could send some of the crew over to help clear up.'

'Thanks for the offer, Doug, but we're fine,' Cassie said. 'Where are you?'

Doug spent so much time on business trips, she was never quite sure where he was.

'Brittany. I wanted to ask you to pencil a date in your diary.'

Cassie waited.

'Normally all my business dinners are in London and Vanessa acts as my hostess.'

There was a hesitant pause before Doug continued.

'I've got an important awards dinner coming up in Cornwall and I know Vanessa is unavailable. Cassie, would you consider being my partner and hostess for the evening?'

'Oh, Doug, I don't know if I'm up to business dinners.'

'I really would love to have you at my side for the evening, Cassie,' he persisted.

'Where's it being held? And what's the date?'

'Royal Carlton.' Doug named the most prestigious hotel and conference centre in the region. 'The eighteenth of next month.'

Cassie gulped. The Royal Carlton?

'May I think about it, Doug? It's not really my scene . . . '

'Cassie, I need a partner for the evening and I would love it to be you.

'And, of course, as this is a business dinner, all expenses will be on me. I'll even treat you to a new frock, if you like.

'I'm back on *Megabyte* at the end of the week, so come for supper one evening and let me know then.'

*   *   *

A week later, Cassie drove into town to see Anna. Glebe House was virtually finished and Anna was keen to give Cassie the guided tour.

'I've put a couple of chairs in the summerhouse. I thought we'd have coffee down there. How's the cleaning up after the fire going?'

'We're nearly finished. Dad's a bit depressed. The thieves got away with more than he'd originally reckoned and the insurance company are querying everything. But things should be back to normal soon. I just hope they catch the culprits.'

'Any developments on that front?'

'Cassie shook her head.

'No. They're working on the theory the thieves used a small boat that they keep hidden somewhere. James has been doing a detailed inventory of all the small boats he sees on the river and inspecting the smaller creeks for any hidden craft.'

'How is James?'

'Fine, I think. Lara has agreed to me using her yacht, *It's Mine!* while she's away and I've entered a couple of races in the local regatta. James is crewing for me. That is, if he's calmed down and forgiven me. I haven't plucked up the courage yet to phone him.'

Anna raised her eyebrows enquiringly.

'Last time I saw him we had a blazing row,' Cassie explained.

'What about?'

Cassie looked at her friend wryly.

'Doug persuaded me to attend an important business dinner with him next month — all expenses paid, including a new evening dress. James is furious.'

'I suppose he's jealous.' Anna smiled gently.

'Yes, possibly a bit,' Cassie conceded. 'But he also thinks Doug is using me, and he hates the thought of him buying me an expensive outfit. I ended up telling him it was none of his business.'

'Which it isn't, is it?' Anna said.

Cassie shook her head. She took a sip of her coffee before replying.

'Actually, I'm not comfortable with

accepting the new outfit offer, either. Hotel and travel expenses are one thing, but clothes . . . ' She shook her head doubtfully.

'Anyway, the whole thing has upset James and I'm really sorry about that. Honestly, life was a lot simpler when I just stayed at home.'

'Maybe. But you weren't really living then, were you?' Anna pointed out quietly.

Cassie smiled.

'True. It took me a long time to realise it, though.' She stood up and put her cup on the tray.

'Thanks for the coffee. I'd better be getting back. Now, are you sure about coming up to the boatyard while Tom and Mai are in London?'

'Positive. How's Tom coping now the plaster is off?'

'Fine. His legs are weak, of course, but he's got lots of exercises to do. The biggest problem is making him take it slowly. He's desperate to get back into the swing of things. And both of them are looking forward to their break.'

'I'll see you bright and early Tuesday morning then,' Anna said. 'And, Cassie, phone James and clear the air.'

Making Up — And Kissing

By Tuesday morning, however, Cassie still hadn't contacted James. She was feeling very guilty and knew that her apology was overdue.

Having taken Tom and Mai to the station to catch the ten o'clock London train, she decided to call in at his office on her way back.

James greeted her with a big smile.

'Cassie, I was going to ring. Come in and have a coffee.'

'James, I wanted to apologise,' Cassie began, but he interrupted.

'I'm the one who should be apologising. I over-reacted,' he said. 'Much as I would like it to be my business, as you pointed out, who you see has nothing to do with me.'

'I'm really sorry I've upset you,' Cassie said. 'I know it's because you care and are concerned for me.'

James brushed her words aside.

'Do you still want me to crew for you this weekend?' he asked instead.

'Please. I can't possibly manage without you.'

The look of longing in James's eyes at her words brought a flush to Cassie's cheeks. What on earth was she thinking of, upsetting such a lovely man?

Impulsively, she went across and gave him a gentle kiss.

'James, you are a very special friend.'

'You know I want more than that, Cassie,' James said quietly and drew her towards him in a tight hug.

'This is not the place to tell you again how I feel, but you know I'm always here for you.'

His unexpected kiss was not as gentle as the one she'd given him, but Cassie found herself relaxing into his embrace.

When James reluctantly let her go, Cassie changed the subject.

'Any news on the job front?'

'I should hear this week about the redundancy package they're prepared to offer me. Then it's decision time.'

A buzz and flashing light on the office intercom caught his attention.

'Excuse me, Cassie.' James picked up his internal phone.

He listened intently.

'I'll be with you in about fifteen minutes,' he said, then turned to Cassie.

'I'm sorry, I'll have to go. There's been an incident up river. Your burglars are possibly involved.'

Cassie opened his office door.

'Take care, James. I'll see you on board *It's Mine!* on Saturday. Eight o'clock, OK?'

'Oh, I'll be in touch before then. And I'll let you know if there are any developments as far as your burglary is concerned.' A quick peck on her cheek and he was running downstairs towards the quay and his launch.

Watching him go, Cassie felt a surge

of affection for him. She really regretted hurting him over Doug and this dinner dance.

Fleetingly, she considered telling Doug she'd changed her mind, but decided against it.

The misunderstanding between herself and James had been cleared up and they were friends again, which was all that mattered.

* * *

Twelve thousand miles away in the Southern Ocean, Lara was struggling to bring *Clotted Cream* alongside Jean-Paul's stricken yacht.

A change of wind direction had delayed her arrival by a couple of hours and now the same wind was hampering the rescue operation itself.

As she struggled in the large swell that was rocking both yachts, she was very aware of how ill Jean-Paul looked. He was clearly in no fit state to give her much assistance. Judging

267

by his greeting, he still had his sense of humour, though.

'Hi, Little Lara. What kept you?'

Standing on *Clotted Cream's* deck trying to judge the right moment for throwing a line across to the other yacht, she could hear the ominous sound of the damaged keel banging. That could mean only one thing.

Water would be seeping slowly into the hull and it could only be a matter of time before the yacht sank. They needed to work fast.

Somehow she was going to have to haul Jean-Paul aboard *Clotted Cream* despite his obvious injuries.

Several waterproof bags were lying on the floor of the cockpit. Jean-Paul had stowed as much of his gear as possible, including his laptop and yacht's log. Now, as Lara threw him the line, he clumsily tied bags on to it ready to be hauled across the heaving gap between the two boats.

At last Jean-Paul gave her a thumbs-up sign.

'Winch away!' he yelled.

Minutes later his dripping possessions were on the floor of *Clotted Cream*'s cabin, having safely survived being dragged through the water. Lara looked across at Jean-Paul.

'You're next. Unless you fancy swimming?'

His reply was blown away in a gust of wind, but he began the difficult task of hooking his safety harness on to the line.

Pain

The heavy swell was lifting both yachts, not in unison but one after the other. Lara wished the gap between the yachts was smaller but it was impossible in these huge seas. For a heart-stopping moment, as she slowly winched him across, Jean-Paul disappeared when a huge swell engulfed him.

Forcing herself to keep on turning the winch, she willed him to reappear and allowed herself a small sigh of relief when she saw the orange flash of his lifejacket.

Turning the winch as quickly as she could, she watched as the line pulled Jean-Paul ever closer to *Clotted Cream* and the point where she would finally be able to haul him on board.

Half an hour later, they both collapsed on the deck of *Clotted Cream* — Lara from sheer exhaustion and Jean-Paul from the huge amount of pain he was in.

Lara tried to assess his injuries and handed him some painkillers.

'Here, take these and let me see if I can do something about that gash on your leg. Not to mention your hand.'

Jean-Paul swallowed the tablets.

'I'm eternally grateful,' he said quietly. 'Thanks, Lara.'

'Hey, they're only tablets,' Lara was about to say, when she realised that he was thanking her for rescuing him. Embarrassed, she patted him on the shoulder instead.

He flinched in pain.

'I think I've broken my shoulder, too,' he said.

'I'll let Race HQ know you're on board and see if they know when the frigate is likely to arrive. Their doctor will soon sort you out. But first I'll put the coffee on,' Lara said. 'I think we both deserve a cup. I might just put a splash of my emergency brandy in it!'

11

'Regrets'?

'Will you cope all right with these steps?' Mai looked anxiously at Tom. 'I think so. I'm getting used to trusting my legs again and not leaning on a crutch.' Tom grinned at her.

'Anyway, there's a handrail.' He gratefully hauled himself up towards the theatre restaurant where he and Mai had plans to enjoy a leisurely meal before the play's evening performance began.

It was the last day of their break and Tom knew that Mai had enjoyed the bright lights and bustle of city life.

When they'd met and fallen in love last year, he'd told her about the sleepy corner of the West Country he came from. She'd laughed and confessed to being an out and out townie.

'Mai, you don't have any regrets, do you?'

'Regrets? What sort?' Mai sounded surprised.

'Marrying me. Living in the country. Giving up all this.'

'Tom, I love you. Where you are is where I want to be. Sure, I did miss the social life initially. But I've made lots of friends back home now, and I feel really settled at the boatyard.' She paused and looked at him.

'It's the first time I've ever had much of a home life. That more than compensates for any lack of shops or entertainment.'

She reached out and held his hand across the table.

'My life has never been this good. And now you've recovered from your accident and the baby is due to put in an appearance soon, it can only get better.

'You know . . . ' But whatever else Mai was going to say was lost as somebody at the bar caught her attention.

'Isn't that Sebastian over there?'

Tom looked around.

'Yes, it is. Mum said he was due back in the UK now his exercise is over. I'm surprised he hasn't been in touch. Shall I ask him to join us?'

Mai shook her head.

'No. Best not. I think he's got company.'

Tom shifted slightly in his chair and they both watched as Sebastian affectionately kissed a tall brunette and put a proprietary arm around her shoulders. Moments later, the couple left the bar and vanished into the theatre auditorium.

Mai looked at Tom.

'Mmm. What do you make of that, then?'

But Tom was speechless.

Emotional Reunion

'Cassie, quick! Lara's on the news! They're carrying a report of her arrival in New Zealand. They're going to show her rescue video, too,' James called out as he turned up the volume on the TV.

It was Saturday evening and Cassie and James had returned to the cottage after competing with *It's Mine!* in the local regatta. They were very pleased with themselves, having come in third.

Now, they watched the TV footage of the harbour-side crowded with people waving flags and cheering to welcome Lara. Then the cameras swung across to the official launch for a close-up of Jean-Paul. One shoulder was heavily strapped and his right wrist was in plaster, but there was a broad smile on his face.

'This is a man who is determined to welcome Little Lara to New Zealand and to say thank you publicly,' the commentator's voice continued.

'Rescued by Lara and then flown here to New Zealand by the Australian Navy for urgent medical treatment, Jean-Paul has spent the last few days anticipating his saviour's arrival. He's had time to relive these scenes and to reflect on how lucky he is to be alive.'

The pictures of cheering crowds faded into Lara's video.

Cassie watched in silence. Looking at the huge seas and the way the two yachts were at the mercy of the elements, she realised Lara had played down the whole incident when she'd spoken to her. The rescue had been a lot more dangerous than she'd let on.

Cassie swallowed hard, but the lump in her throat refused to go away and the tears started to trickle down her cheeks.

James moved across and took her in his arms.

'It's over, Cassie. She did it and now she's safe in New Zealand. Look at the crowds. They love her. She's the heroine of the day.'

As the rescue video finished, the cameras went back to witness live the emotional reunion between Jean-Paul and Lara.

'Thanks, Little Lara. I owe you.' Jean-Paul held her tight.

'*Clotted Cream* and Lara now have

to spend the statutory three days here in port before leaving to try to catch up with the rest of the fleet. During this time, Lara will sleep as much as she can and her shore crew will be preparing the yacht not only for the Southern Ocean but also the notorious Cape Horn.'

The commentator went on to discuss how Lara's final position would be affected by the time spent rescuing Jean-Paul.

'Because of the handicapping system, Lara will have to finish the next two legs in higher than seventh place to achieve a podium position. We wish her well.'

Surprise

As the report finished and the programme reverted to domestic news, the telephone in the cottage rang.

James was nearest and he automatically picked it up. He smiled at the note of surprise he detected in the caller's voice.

'James? It's Tom. Have you got the TV on? Lara seems to be on every channel! We've recorded one report just in case Mum missed it.'

'I'm sure she'll be pleased about that. We've just seen the rescue video on the news,' James said.

'Do you want a word with Cassie?'

'No, don't worry. I'll catch up with her tomorrow. Sorry for interrupting your evening.' Tom hung up quickly, leaving James amused.

'I think Tom was surprised to hear my voice,' he said to Cassie. 'You didn't tell him I was coming to supper after the race?'

Cassie shook her head.

'No. I didn't feel the need. Besides, I've barely seen him since he and Mai got back from London yesterday. I haven't even had the chance to tell him about the lead on the burglars.'

'We're not too sure about that, yet,' James warned. 'It isn't enough simply to be convinced that the men who were arrested last week are also responsible for the break-in and fire at the boatyard.

'We need hard evidence before we can charge them. I know the police are hopeful that Forensics will be able to come up with matching finger and footprints.'

'When will they have the results?' Cassie asked.

'Some time this week. Then the police will decide whether to press charges or not.' James sighed.

'Crime on the river is becoming a real problem — and the merging of the two Harbour Master jobs isn't going to help.' He looked at her.

'I shall be glad to hand over the responsibility to someone else.'

'When are the changes likely to come into effect?' Cassie asked.

'Some time after the end of the season. They want me to stay on for a month to hand things over to the new chap. And that will be the end of my official working life,' he said pensively.

'Look on it as an adventure.' Cassie smiled. 'It could be exciting.'

'Perhaps you're right. Maybe I should think about moving to another area, but I really like it around here. I definitely like the company.'

The look in his eyes made Cassie blush.

Before he could say more, Cassie spoke quickly.

'Finish your coffee, James. I'm going to turn you out in about five minutes. I'm whacked after all that fresh air and exercise. I need an early night.' She deliberately kept her tone light.

James sighed as he watched her carry his empty coffee cup through to the kitchen. He picked up his jacket, then kissed her lightly on the cheek.

'Thanks for a good day. I'll give you a ring in the morning.'

Without another word he was gone, the door closing behind him with a sharp click.

Lara's Journal

Saturday 18th.

The rest of the fleet left New Zealand ten days before I arrived and are now well ahead of me. Colin on Flight of the Seagull is currently in the lead — again — and the others are spread out behind him.

This leg has already given me some difficult sailing. I know there's still more to come if I'm to finish in a decent position in Brazil.

It's raining hard at the moment with some tremendous seas out there and I'm very tired.

Getting only three days' rest in New Zealand instead of the three weeks everybody else got didn't give me enough time to regain my strength.

I'd hoped by sailing a slightly northern course I'd find some better weather, but so far that hasn't worked.

Everyone warned me this would be the toughest leg of the race, and the closer I get to Cape Horn the more I realise how right they were.

Two days ago I sailed through an iceberg field.

Seeing those immense, towering lumps of ice was an awesome experience. Considering the consequences of Clotted Cream connecting with one of them, however, was a sobering thought.

I've never felt so alone and so vulnerable in my life.

It took me hours to navigate my way through the ice field and away from all the dangerously loose floating growlers that had broken off. Finally I passed my last berg — the largest of them all. Its menacing beauty was breathtaking.

I feel absolutely drained now. All that concentration and lack of sleep has taken its toll.

Dexter phoned before I started to write this and he insisted that I get some sleep.

'You have the Cape to face in a few days. You're going to need all your *strength for that. And remember, Lara, I'm rooting for you. Please take care.'*

★   ★   ★

Cassie stood in front of the hotel mirror and surveyed her appearance. For a woman who'd just passed a milestone birthday she didn't think she looked too bad.

Anna had been right about the dress. It was perfect.

Cassie had felt distinctly guilty about spending such a large amount of money on one dress. However, having refused to allow Doug to buy her an outfit for the occasion, the bill was all hers.

She smoothed a stray strand of hair back into place, pleased with the new highlights.

She'd just attached the second of her favourite pearl stud earrings when there was a quiet knock on the door.

'Cassie, it's time we went downstairs,'

Doug called from outside.

'Come in. I'm ready. Will I do?'

Doug, looking debonair in his tuxedo, smiled at her before taking her in his arms and gently kissing her.

'You look beautiful. The guys are going to be so jealous of me this evening.'

'I hope I don't let you down. I'm not used to businessmen *en masse*.' Cassie moved out of his arms and picked up her bag.

'Cassie, they'll love you. Don't worry.'

He glanced at her wrist.

'You're not wearing the bracelet I gave you for your birthday.' He sounded disappointed.

'I didn't think the amber stones went with this dress,' Cassie explained quickly. 'It really needs silver and I don't possess a silver bracelet.

'But the amber is in my case, if you'd like me to wear it.'

Doug shook his head.

'No, you're right. It doesn't go.

'Oh, Cassie, I'm just so pleased you

agreed to come this evening.' He caught hold of her hand and raised it to his lips.

Inquisition

Downstairs, they crossed the foyer and joined the throng making their way slowly into the large ballroom.

There was already a couple seated at their table. With his arm possessively around Cassie's waist, Doug made the introductions.

'Josie, Ben, this is Cassie, a very special friend of mine. I'd be grateful if you'd look after her for me while I make a quick phone call.'

He turned to Cassie.

'I won't be long.'

It was only a matter of minutes before the rest of their party joined them and Cassie found her head swimming with the effort of trying to remember which name went with which face.

A man who introduced himself as Edwin sat in the empty seat on her right. Apparently he was Doug's technical right-hand man.

He and his wife also seemed to regard themselves as having some sort of proprietary right over Doug, and when Josie introduced Cassie as a special friend of Doug's, both sets of eyebrows went up and the inquisition began.

'How long have you known Dougie, then?' Edwin asked.

'Where did you meet?' his wife wanted to know.

Cassie took a deep breath before replying, keeping her answers brief. Then she smiled at Edwin.

'And you, how long have you known Doug?' she countered.

'For ever. I was best man at his wedding. My wife's godmother to both the girls. Vanessa's usually with Doug at these functions.'

Josie, who clearly thought Edwin was out of order, tried to stem the flow of questions, but Edwin simply ignored her and carried on cross-examining Cassie.

'How long have you been a widow?'

'Twenty years. How long have you been married?'

'It's our pearl anniversary this year,' Edwin said smugly, looking at his wife.

'Congratulations,' Cassie said, wondering what the next personal question would be.

Looking around, she was relieved to see Doug making his way back towards them and she pointedly turned away from Edwin.

'More Than Friendship'

If Doug noticed the strained atmosphere between Cassie and his 'right-hand-man', he made no comment.

Inevitably there was a lot of business talk around the table as they ate, but Doug made a point of including Cassie.

When dinner and the short awards ceremony were over, the tables were cleared and disco music began to fill the air. The doors leading out on to the terrace were opened and people began to circulate.

Doug stood up and held his hand out to Cassie.

'I need some fresh air. Will you join me on the terrace?'

Once outside, Doug turned to Cassie.

'I always seem to be apologising to you,' he said. 'Josie tells me Edwin gave you the third degree.'

'Your family and friends are obviously very protective of you,' Cassie said diplomatically.

Doug sighed.

'What none of them seems to realise is the amount of time I spend on my own these days. Edwin goes home to his family. Vanessa — well, Vanessa is a popular girl and leads a busy social life.

'For me, after work it's invariably either a TV dinner or a hotel meal, alone.' He looked at Cassie.

'I realise we haven't known each

other long, but I'm already very fond of you. I want you to know I'm offering more than friendship.'

Cassie felt herself blush under the intensity of his look.

'Doug, I . . . ' She took a deep breath, before continuing.

'I've been on my own for so long, it's difficult for me, too. I've only just started to venture outside of the world I'd hidden in for so long. I need time to sort things out before I make any commitment to anyone.'

'So long as you're not frightened away even before we begin.' He leaned forward and gently brushed her fore-head with his lips.

'I have a small thank-you present for you.' He reached into the inside pocket of his dinner jacket.

The twisted bands of silver made an unusual bracelet.

Cassie looked at him in surprise.

'Where did you get this? And when?'

'The hotel shop was still open. I couldn't resist it. I hope you like it. It certainly goes with your dress.'

'Doug, I wasn't hinting.'

'Shh. I know. No protests. Like I said, it's a thank-you present.' This time he pulled her into his arms and kissed her properly.

He smiled as he released her.

'Cassie, we're going to make a great couple.'

★ ★ ★

Sunday afternoon saw Cassie pacing the floor of the cottage, trying to put worrying thoughts of Lara out of her mind. Dexter had rung earlier to say that Lara was a bit low. She was due to call any moment.

'Maybe talking to you will do the trick,' Dexter had said to Cassie.

He was already in Brazil, waiting for the yachts to arrive, and was clearly concerned.

'Once she arrives in Brazil I can give her all the TLC she needs, but right now she's feeling very vulnerable.'

When the telephone rang Cassie grabbed the receiver.

'Lara?'

'Hi, Mum. Got time to talk?' The tension in Lara's voice was obvious.

'Are you all right, love?' Cassie asked, forcing herself to keep calm. 'Has something happened?'

'No. Nothing. I just need to talk to you.'

Cassie stiffened when she heard the desperation in Lara's tone.

'Mum, I think I'm cracking up,' Lara wailed. 'I'm not cut out to be a solo sailor. I'm exhausted, fed up with my own company and I'm going to let everyone down.

'There's no way I'm going to win the race, even if I do manage to sail round Cape Horn and get to Brazil. The whole thing has been a pointless exercise. I just want to come home.'

Her sobs travelled down the line in great gulps.

Cassie took a deep breath.

'Now, you listen to me, Lara Lewis.

You're the one who was determined to do this race. You're the one who badgered everyone into agreeing to give you the chance. And you're the one who will see it through. Do you understand?'

'We All Love You'

Cassie sensed rather than heard Lara swallowing her sobs, trying to regulate her breathing.

'The fact you won't win the race has nothing to do with anything. What is important is that you've tried, you've done your best. And more. Lara, you saved a man's life. Winning any race has to take second place to that. Now, how much sleep have you had recently?'

'Catnaps.'

Cassie was silent. With Cape Horn looming, it was extremely unlikely that Lara would get more than catnaps for the foreseeable future. If she could only hove to and get a couple of hours' decent sleep, she might see things in a better perspective.

'How far are you from Cape Horn?'

'About two hundred miles.'

'Well, I suggest you increase both your catnaps and your food intake. Try to get some strength back.

'Have you spoken to Dexter or Tom recently? They've both done a lot of single-handed sailing. They'll know much better than me what you're going through. Keep talking to them.' Cassie paused.

'And Lara, remember we all love you. We're all proud of your achievements so far and we know you can do it. Get to Brazil and see how you feel then.'

The delayed action of the satellite phone seemed to accentuate the tension. The sigh that travelled down the line was as deep as ever. Cassie held her breath. Had her pep-talk worked?

'Mum, I'm sorry, but I don't think I can carry on.'

The connection died.

12

'A Sudden Decision'

Cassie and James were enjoying a coffee after supper, sitting on the tiny flower-filled patio of River View Cottage. A lingering smell of honeysuckle filled the air, and in the quiet of the evening all they could hear was the gentle lapping of the river and the occasional call of a homeward-bound curlew.

Cassie glanced at James, thinking how much a part of her life he was now and how much she enjoyed his quiet uncomplicated company and the things they did together — sailing, theatre visits and simple suppers together like this evening.

It was all so different to the hectic, social life Doug was introducing her to.

James caught her glance.

'Are you OK?' he asked quietly.

Cassie nodded.

'I'm fine. If I'm honest, I haven't been this good in years.'

During the last few weeks their relationship had slipped effortlessly on to a new level. She'd been so worried about Lara, and his support had been tireless.

Sitting here companionably together, Cassie was suddenly overwhelmed with the desire to tell him how much he meant to her. But before she could say a word. James spoke.

'You've turned this place into a real home, Cassie. I love coming here.' He looked around appreciatively.

'Mind you, I love the company too.'

Cassie knew that he spoke the simple truth. She could see it in his eyes. He did love her.

He raised his hands in resignation.

'Sorry Cassie. I promised myself I wouldn't push you.'

'James. I . . .'

He shook his head.

'You like living on your own, then? You're not lonely?' Even to his own ears James sounded wistful.

Cassie smiled.

'I've really enjoyed setting up home here and I don't have time to be lonely. What with work at the boatyard, sailing with you, helping Tom and Mai out, seeing to Anna, walking Solo, not to mention all the suppers we have together,' she teased, 'time flies by.'

'Then there are all the social events Doug invites me to.'

She ignored the grimace that crossed James's face at the mention of Doug. He'd made his feelings clear about that association.

Cassie knew he was unhappy on the days she went out with Doug, but she couldn't deny the fact she enjoyed the luxurious side of life Doug had introduced her to recently. It was exciting.

'My life has turned into something of a social whirl. Changed days.' She bent down to stroke Solo, who was lying at their feet.

There was a short silence before James spoke.

'Cassie, I'm leaving in a few days for a holiday in Wales.'

'That's a sudden decision, isn't it?' Cassie sounded surprised.

James shrugged.

'I thought I might as well take the last of my holiday entitlement, I need to think about my future, too. I don't suppose there's any chance of you coming with me, is there?'

Cassie shook her head.

'You know I've got a golf charity tournament with Doug at the end of the week.'

'Will you come up afterwards? No, of course not.' James tersely answered his own question.

There was a strained silence for several seconds.

'James, I'm sorry, but I did promise Doug I'd go,' Cassie said eventually.

James stood up.

'I've got an early start in the office tomorrow. I'm trying to tie up as many loose ends as I can. Walk to the launch with me?'

'Of course.'

Cassie knew he was upset.

'James, I'll miss you while you're away,' she said, trying to make amends with the truth. 'Will you phone me from Wales?'

'Of course.'

The evening air was cooler down by the river with a breeze coming up off the water, and Cassie shivered involuntarily.

James hesitantly turned towards Cassie before taking her in his arms.

'Don't get cold.' He held her tightly for a moment or two.

'While I'm away, will you please think about us, Cassie? About our relationship, and where it's going? I'd like to plan a future that includes you and me together. I can't wait much longer. You're going to have to decide what you want.'

He drew her towards him and kissed her gently.

'I love you, Cassie. Please marry me.'

Lara's Journal

Saturday 15th.
The idea of this journal was to keep a truthful record of my private thoughts and fears during the race. So with that in mind, I'm going to try to write as rationally and as honestly as I can about the events of the past few weeks.

Cape Horn is finally behind me.

Two days on from that grey outcrop with its fearsome reputation, and I was in a different world. The days were beautiful — blue sky, sunshine and a real 'great to be alive' feeling in the air.

I think Clotted Cream sensed we'd literally turned a corner because she started to skim across the water as though she, too, was happy to be back in the Atlantic Ocean. And now, in a few days, Brazil beckons.

I hope, when I think about this adventure in years to come, I can recapture not only the memory of the good days but also the sheer terror of the time I spent in this part of the Southern Ocean.

If nothing else, it will serve to remind me that having survived this I should be able to survive anything life can throw at me.

I definitely owe Mum a big hug and the biggest box of chocolates I can buy when I get back. I was way out of order, ringing her like that. I feel so guilty for hanging up on her, just because I didn't want to acknowledge the truth of what she was saying.

It's no excuse, I know, but at the time I wasn't thinking straight. I was so exhausted. Being so tired was terrifying in itself, without the tumultuous weather conditions I had to contend with.

Talking to Mum may have been upsetting for her, but it was the best thing possible for me.

Dexter rang me a few minutes after

my outburst with Mum. He, too, was quite brutal and matter-of-fact.

'Lara, you have no choice. Just get on with it and stop moaning.'

I'd never heard such a steely edge to his voice before. He's always encouraged me, but in a much gentler way. This time he definitely sounded cross.

'By the way, I have some news for you about future sponsorship. I'll tell you about it in Brazil. That is if you haven't lost your bottle for yacht racing.' There was a pause before he went on more gently.

'I know it's tough out there, Lara, but you can cope. And don't forget, I'm here waiting for you.'

I guess I owe Dexter as much as Mum because it was their united onslaught that made me pull myself together.

It was forty-eight hours before I felt in control again. Three hours later I was on course for rounding Cape Horn. I was approximately two miles from the rock when I passed it.

The light was spectacular. Watching the massive Southern Ocean breakers slam against the steep rocky buttresses of the island sent tingles of adrenalin down my spine.

After passing safely through one of the world's most dangerous areas I remember breathing a huge sigh of relief and feeling a wave of euphoria sweep over me.

Only another eight thousand nautical miles to go and I'll be home. I have to hang on to that feeling.

According to Race HQ this morning, I'm currently in ninth position, which puts me way down in the points, but at least I'm still in there fighting. I'll be on the start line, too, with the others for the next leg, not racing to try to catch up.

★ ★ ★

Cassie was spending the night with Anna at Glebe House, ready for an early start the next day. Doug was collecting them at seven a.m. to drive them to the country club for the golf tournament. He'd drawn an early place in the competition.

'You and Doug seem to be close, these days,' Anna observed as she filled the kettle.

'He's good fun and we enjoy each other's company,' Cassie answered. 'But that's as far as it goes — on my side, anyway.'

Anna raised her eyebrows, but Cassie refused to be drawn further so Anna changed the subject.

'Have you told Lara yet about Tom seeing Sebastian in London?'

'Yes. She just said it was one less thing for her to worry about. It stopped her feeling guilty about breaking things off with him when she gets back. I must say I'm relieved. I never could quite see Lara as a Naval wife.'

Anna handed Cassie a mug of hot chocolate.

'Have you heard from James?' she asked.

'He rang to say he'd arrived in Wales

safely. I thought he'd call this evening, but . . . ' Cassie shrugged her shoulders philosophically.

'There's still time,' Anna said, glancing at the clock.

'Has he decided what he's going to do when he finishes at the Harbour Commission?'

'No, not yet. He's got several options but can't decide which one to take. That's what this holiday is about — in part. He needs time to do some serious thinking without any distractions — including me.'

Cassie hadn't told Anna about James's proposal.

Anna looked questioningly at her. 'You?'

'James has asked me to marry him.'

'And you said?' Anna prompted.

'I'm thinking about it. He wants my answer when he gets back.' Cassie sighed.

'I know he loves me. And I think I love him. He makes me laugh and we're . . . we're comfortable together.' She paused.

'It's just my heart doesn't miss a beat the way it used to whenever I saw Miles. And I can't help wondering whether I love him enough.'

'Miles was a long time ago,' Anna said quietly. 'You were both young. Second time around is bound to be different, but that doesn't make it any less real. James adores you. Anybody can see that from the way he looks at you when he thinks no-one else is watching.'

'The problem is I've been on my own for so long and what I had with Miles was so good, I dread making a mistake.'

'Are you sure Doug and the kind of life he could offer isn't clouding your judgment?' Anna asked hesitantly.

Cassie shook her head.

'Definitely not. I like Doug a lot and the social whirl of the last few months has been fun. But you know me, I'm a home bird really.' She looked at Anna.

'I've already decided that after tomorrow's tournament I'm going to do a bit of back-pedalling as far as invitations from Doug are concerned.'

'Talking of tomorrow, I think it's time we went to bed. We've got an early start.'

'Injured'

By lunchtime the following day it was clear that the charity golf tournament was going to be a success. Good weather and an enthusiastic turnout of local business people ensured the local charities would all benefit from large donations.

Cassie watched Doug and then Anna tee off before making for the club's health and beauty rooms. She'd never been a golfer and was treating herself to a massage and a facial before returning downstairs to wait for everyone to come in for lunch.

Accepting the offer of a glass of orange juice from one of the waiters, she wandered across to the terrace. A radio somewhere in the background was tuned into a local station and Cassie could hear the DJ urging everyone to 'Get yourself over to the country club and play a round for charity.'

Lunch was a lavish buffet and as Doug, Anna and Cassie began to help themselves, the radio switched to a news bulletin.

'And now for news of a local hero,' Cassie heard the newsreader say. 'Whilst on holiday in Wales, Captain James White, a harbour master at one of our ports down here, has been injured while saving the life of a three-year-old toddler.'

As her plate silently hit the carpeted floor Cassie fought the nausea that threatened to overwhelm her, and she struggled to remain upright. Anna was at her side in an instant.

'Cassie, are you all right?'

Cassie nodded.

'Listen.'

'The three-year-old ran into a busy road and the captain followed, scooping her out of the way of oncoming traffic. Captain White took the brunt of the impact from a speeding van and is now in hospital.'

As music signalled the end of the bulletin, Cassie turned to Doug.

'I must go to him. I'm sorry to leave, Doug, but . . . '

'Cassie, I understand,' he interrupted. 'I'll get someone to take you home to collect some things first and then drive you to the station.'

Doug's matter-of-fact way of handling the situation was his way of coping. He did understand. He understood she was sorry to leave, and also that their relationship had unexpectedly undergone a significant change.

'I'm sorry, Doug,' she said again.

'I know, Cassie. We'll talk later. Go and see how James is. And remember, if there's anything I can do, ask me.'

'A Life Of Her Own'

Tom took the call from the police in the boatyard office. Fully mobile again, he was spending a lot of time with Bill, becoming increasingly involved in the family business.

'Sergeant Winston here. We've got the results from the forensic department and there's enough evidence to charge the three suspects with burglary and arson.'

'That's great news. Thanks for letting us know, Sergeant.'

Bill looked at him as he replaced the receiver.

'Finally doing something, are they? Good. I don't suppose the courts will give 'em more than community service but there you are. It won't bring back what the fire damaged either.'

'No,' Tom agreed, 'but it could have been a lot worse. At least the insurance have finally agreed a figure so we can start replacing tools, get back into the boat maintenance business and try to recoup the business we've lost over the last few weeks.'

He glanced at his grandfather.

'I've had an idea about that, too.'

Bill held up his hands in mock horror.

'Here we go again. You and your modern ideas. What now?' he asked good-naturedly.

'Why don't we set up a website to attract more business into the yard?' Tom said.

'Beats me how a website can attract new business. In my day it was a question of building up a reputation for good work,' Bill grumbled. 'But you go ahead if you think it's what's needed.

'Watch the expense side of it, mind. You'll need to talk to your mother about available funds when she gets back from Wales.'

Tom glanced at his grandfather.

'Gramps, what do you make of Mum rushing off like that?' he said slowly.

'I reckon it's a good sign.'

'Sign of what?'

'That your mum is finally getting a life of her own,' Bill said, looking directly at Tom.

'I thought she had a life of her own. She always seems happy, and she's got a busy social life, too, these days. And I know she's looking forward to being a grandmother.'

Bill nodded.

'All that's true. But it's been a long time since there was anyone special in her life. Now it looks as though James might be about to fill the void.

'Things change,' he added, giving his grandson a sympathetic look. 'Your dad will always be her first love, but your gran and I always hoped he wouldn't be her last.'

*   *   *

Walking down the hospital corridor, Cassie felt unsure of herself and full of fear, in spite of the reassurance the ward sister had given her over the telephone.

'Captain White doesn't have any life-threatening injuries. He's very bruised, he's sprained an ankle and a couple of his ribs are broken. We kept him in overnight for observation and he'll be discharged some time today.

'It was a brave thing he did. He's lucky to have got off so lightly.'

As she pushed open the swing door of the hospital ward, Cassie prepared herself for an emotional meeting.

At first, she couldn't see James. Then her heart skipped a beat when she finally spotted him sitting talking to an elderly man.

It was his companion who nudged him and pointed Cassie out to James.

'You've got a visitor.'

As James turned, a smile of sheer delight crossed his face and he struggled to stand up.

'No, no, James, be careful,' Cassie said, kissing him gently.

'What am I going to do with you? I

let you out of my sight for a day and you play Superman.'

'He's a real hero,' James's companion said, standing up to shake Cassie's hand.

'I'm Ivor, grandfather of the toddler he saved. I can't tell you how grateful the family are. We'll always be in the captain's debt.'

James looked embarrassed.

'Well, now that your wife's here I'll say goodbye. Thank you once again,' Ivor said.

James glanced apologetically at Cassie.

'Oh, Cassie's not . . . ' he started to explain. Then he saw the look on her face and stopped mid-sentence.

'Goodbye, Ivor. Take care of that granddaughter of yours. She's very precious,' James said, still looking at Cassie in amazement.

Before either of them could say anything, the ward sister bustled up.

'How are you feeling? The doctor's on his way to discharge you, Captain White.'

'I've never felt better,' James said,

reaching out for Cassie's hand and holding it tightly. 'Never better.'

'You're The One I Want'

It was nine o'clock that evening before Cassie rang Boatyard House.

Mai had gone up for an early night and it was Tom who answered.

'Hi, Mum. How are things? Is James going to be OK?'

'He's bruised and battered, but otherwise fine. How's Mai?'

'A bit tired. She's finding moving around difficult.'

'Give her my love.'

'I will.'

'Listen, Tom, we're going to stay up here for a couple of days. James has still got his hotel booking and they've found a room for me. The idea is for James to rest for a while, give the bruises time to fade, and then I'll drive him home.'

'Sounds like a good idea. Solo's fine. She's taken to sleeping on the floor of the nursery. And Mum — ' Tom hesitated before adding ' — you know we all like James, don't you?'

Cassie tried to keep the laughter out of her voice as she replied.

'Good, I'm glad you told me that, Tom. I like him, too.'

She was still laughing when she rejoined James in the hotel lounge.

'For some reason, completely out of the blue, my son has just told me that they all like you.'

'That's a relief,' James said. 'I shan't have any troubles with the in-laws then.'

'Do you think they've guessed about us?'

'I would think your mercy dash to my side gave them a fair indication of the way things are.' James smiled at her.

'I still can't quite believe you're here,' he added, catching hold of her hand.

'I was sure I was going to lose you to Doug. He has so much more to offer you — a lifestyle that I couldn't possibly begin to compete with.'

Cassie leaned forward and placed a finger against his lips.

'Shh. You're the one I want to be with. Now, I think, considering your condition, you should be tucked up in bed recuperating. We'll talk tomorrow.'

Relief

The customary fireworks and champagne corks were popping as Lara arrived in Brazil.

The official boat took her in tow and they headed towards a berth in the marina where she looked out for Dexter. For a heart-stopping moment she couldn't find him in the crowd, but at last she saw him standing on the quay waiting for her, just as he'd promised.

The moment *Clotted Cream* was tied in her position he leaped on board and hugged her to him.

'Well done, Little Lara!' he exclaimed and she could clearly hear the relief in his voice.

Once the official side of things was over, Dexter walked Lara to her hotel, his arm protectively around her shoulders.

'It's so good to have you here safe and sound. You had me really worried for a while.'

'I'm sorry,' Lara said quietly. 'Forgive me?'

'Of course. I'll see you for supper. I have some news for you, but first you need to rest.'

Three hours later, Lara was sitting next to Dexter in a small café on the waterfront.

'Come on, Dexter, you said you had some news,' Lara said impatiently.

Dexter looked at her thoughtfully as he crumbled his bread roll.

'The first thing is, I've heard unofficially you are about to be offered a sponsorship package in your own name — not as Tom's little sister, or as a stand-in skipper. This deal is for you, Lara Lewis. You've impressed a lot of people during this race.'

When he told her the name of the

sponsor and the huge amount of money they were proposing, Lara was stunned. Her dream of being a professional yacht skipper was about to come true.

'Secondly, the finish of this race in Plymouth will also signal the end of my involvement with the organisation of yacht races. I've decided I want to do more sailing and take part in some of the smaller competitions again.' He took a breath.

'I've also decided to join Dad on the farm.'

'That's great, Dexter. You'll have the best of both worlds — sailing for pleasure and building up a business you enjoy.'

'There is a third thing,' Dexter said, looking at her. 'I had hoped you and I could get together. But the timing is all wrong, isn't it?

'You're about to get your big chance and set the yachting world alight, racing around the globe for the next few years. I'm going to be working equally hard in the heart of the English countryside with the occasional Round Britain yacht race to look forward to.'

'We can still see each other, though, can't we? Your family farm isn't that far from Devon and I won't be on the high seas all the time,' Lara said fearfully.

Dexter took her hand in his.

'Sure, we can try, Little Lara, but I have a feeling it isn't going to be that easy. I don't believe absence always makes the heart grow fonder.' He paused before continuing.

'Sometimes, people get so busy with their individual lives they just drift apart, with regrets on both sides for what might have been.'

13

'Engagement Ring'

Cassie knew that if it hadn't been for his sprained ankle, James would have insisted on driving. As it was, he had no option but to let her get behind the wheel of his precious sports car to take them home.

It was the first time Cassie had ever driven such a fun car and she found herself making the most of it.

'I thought we'd stop for lunch in Bath. I know it's a bit of a detour, but there's a nice convenient restaurant in the city centre.' James smiled enigmatically, refusing to be drawn further.

Traffic was heavy and it was well after one o'clock before Cassie pulled into a carpark.

'There's somewhere we have to go before we eat,' James said.

Holding Cassie's hand tightly and leaning on the walking stick the hospital had loaned him, he led her towards a small shop with a tasteful green and gold blind above its window display of jewellery.

'Come and choose your engagement ring,' James said. 'And meet the friend who I hope will be my best man.'

Charlie Johnson was delighted to see James and gave Cassie a congratulatory hug when he heard their news.

'Now, what sort of rings would you like me to show you? Modern? Traditional? Or perhaps you've already seen something you like?'

A square sapphire in an old-fashioned flat gold setting had caught Cassie's eye and hesitantly she pointed it out. James had given her no idea of how much he wanted to spend and she didn't want to choose a ring he couldn't afford.

'Try it on. I can always alter the size,' Charlie said.

It was then Cassie realised she was

still wearing Miles's wedding ring. She'd never taken it off. It had been a constant reminder of him over the years.

Disconcerted, she slipped off the gold band, replacing it with the sapphire ring, then held out her hand for James to see.

'It's beautiful,' she said. 'Do you like it?' she asked anxiously.

'It's perfect. It looks as if it was made for your hand,' James said. 'We need to choose wedding rings now.'

Some time later, they headed off, leaving two gold wedding bands in Charlie's safe keeping.

'It'll be a privilege to be your best man, James. I'll try not to forget to bring these along on the day!'

★ ★ ★

It was mid evening before they got back to Devon. Cassie left James in his apartment, promising to see him early the next day.

'I love you very much, Cassie.' He

kissed her tenderly.

'Can we please get married as soon as possible?'

Cassie smiled.

'Lara will be home in a couple of weeks. She's going to be my brides-maid, so we'll have to wait for her.'

Once back at River View Cottage, Cassie unpacked her suitcase, before getting ready for bed.

She took off her watch and placed it on the bedside table, glancing at the silver-framed photograph that had stood beside her bed for over twenty years.

She slowly reached out and picked it up, then opened the back and slid out the black and white photo.

It was time to say goodbye. Her finger traced the blurred outline of Miles's face. While photos still brought instant memories, these days she had difficulty in recalling the timbre of his voice. This evening, though, she could definitely hear Miles's soft West Country accent.

Bon voyage, Cassie. Be happy.

Lara's Journal

Wednesday 6th.
This is turning out to be the best leg so far. I think I'm getting the hang of this solo yacht racing!

Not only did I manage to cross the start line in Brazil first, ahead of Colin on Flight of the Seagull, I've held on to the lead for the last fourteen days. Just to think I might be in with a chance of winning this leg makes me want to hoist all the sails I've got.

It won't make any difference to my overall position. I haven't accumulated enough points in the other legs to put me in the top three. That means no podium place, but at least I'll have shown what I'm capable of.

All these weeks at sea have given me lots of time to do some serious thinking about my life. One of my first decisions was not to marry Sebastian.

I think, deep down, I knew when he asked me that it wasn't what I really wanted. Telling him I'd think about it was the coward's way out, but I just didn't have the courage to say 'No' straight off.

When Mum told me Tom and Mai had seen him in London with someone else, all my guilty feelings of not wanting to hurt him vanished.

I rang him from Brazil and told him I'd decided against accepting his proposal. I'm very proud of myself for not mentioning 'the other woman'. Mind you, he didn't say a word about her, either!

We had a very civilised conversation and he even told me I could keep the ring if I wanted to. Of course I won't. At least we parted on friendly terms.

In a few more days I should have Land's End in my sights and then home. The weather systems have been so different from the ones on the way out. Tom helped me plot a different course to pass the Azores and I've made good time.

Dexter has been negotiating with lots of people on my behalf and says I'll have some important decisions to make when I get back.

I've always dreamed about competing in the Vendée Globe and it's still sinking in that the essential sponsorship is finally within my grasp.

However, although this race has been a brilliant experience, if I'm totally honest, I found the weeks of isolation very hard to cope with at times.

The compulsory stopovers at the finish of each leg of this race saved my sanity. Taking part in the non-stop Vendée Globe means being at sea from start to finish — with no outside help of any kind.

Ellen MacArthur took ninety-four days to complete her record voyage, so realistically I'd be looking at nearly three and a half months. I'm not sure I can handle that amount of time on my own at sea.

But it's such a great opportunity. If I turn it down I know it will never be offered again.

Another thing worries me. I know

Dexter and I haven't seen a lot of each other, but I already feel there's a special bond between us.

If I carry on with a solo sailing career I'm afraid I'll lose any chance of that bond growing.

Decisions

James took Cassie back to the stately home where they'd enjoyed the musical evening to celebrate their engagement and to start making plans for their future.

'Shall we get married here?' James asked. 'The private chapel out in the grounds is licensed for weddings now. We could have the reception here as well.'

'That would be lovely,' Cassie said. 'But please can we have a quiet wedding?'

'We could always have a big party in the evening at the country club if you'd like?' James said.

'No. Let's keep it small. Will we have a honeymoon?'

'Of course. And before you ask, I'm not telling you. Just have your passport ready.'

'We'll also have to decide where we're going to live afterwards,' Cassie said.

'The lease on my apartment finishes with my job,' James pointed out. 'I know you love River View Cottage. Do you think it's big enough for both of us? Would Bill sell it?'

'Dad has talked in the past about selling the place so I'm sure that's an option.'

James sighed happily.

'Good. Now all we have to do is decide upon the date. You reckon Lara should be back within the next seven or eight days, so how about two weeks this Saturday?'

'Two weeks this Saturday will be wonderful, James.'

* * *

Life from that evening on became dominated by wedding preparations. Although Cassie dearly wanted to wait until Lara was home so they could shop together for a dress, she didn't dare risk leaving it so late.

Instead, she and Anna spent a delightful day in town, eventually tracking down the perfect wedding dress in an individual shop in one of the small shopping lanes away from the busy town centre. They even found a dress that Cassie knew would be just right for Lara.

To Cassie's embarrassment, as they made their way back to the carpark, they bumped into Doug. She'd wanted to tell Doug about her and James before he heard it on the local grapevine, but had failed to get hold of him.

'Doug, I tried to ring you a couple of days ago,' Cassie began. 'I wanted to tell you something.'

'I've just got back from a business trip. How's James? The last I heard he was recovering in hospital.'

He clearly didn't know about their engagement and Cassie felt bad about breaking her news in such a public place.

'He's home and well on the way to recovery. Doug, I have something to tell you,' Cassie said again, dimly aware that Anna was tactfully moving away.

'James and I are getting married soon.'

There was a fraction of a pause before Doug spoke quietly.

'I wish it were me.'

He kissed her gently on the cheek.

'Congratulations, Cassie. James is a very lucky man. I'm sure you'll be very happy.'

As she watched him walk away Cassie hoped she was imagining the droop in his shoulders.

She sighed. There was nothing she could do. She loved James, not Doug, but she would always remember him and their times together with fondness.

A New Life

When her bedside phone rang in the middle of the night Cassie knew who it was even before she answered it.

'Tom? Is everything all right? Where are you?'

'At the hospital. Mai's contractions started a couple of hours ago. I just wanted to let you know things are happening. I'll ring you again when there's more news.'

'Give Mai my love,' Cassie said.

Half an hour later, having been unable to get back to sleep, Cassie got up.

Waiting for the kettle to boil, she stroked Solo. Sighing contentedly, the dog leaned against her legs.

Taking her mug of coffee outside, Cassie sat on the patio and watched the breaking dawn — a new day and the promise of a brand new life about to start.

She sipped her coffee. Soon, her own new life with James would herald yet more change.

It seemed to Cassie there had been more changes in the past few months than there had been in all the years since Miles had died.

It was another four hours before a tired but happy Tom phoned.

'You'll be pleased to know both mother and baby are doing well, Grandma.'

Cassie breathed a huge sigh of relief.

'The wriggler weighed in at five pounds twelve ounces. And she's beautiful.'

Cassie smiled at the pride in her son's voice.

'Can I visit later?'

'Any time this afternoon. Mai needs to get some rest now.'

Later that morning Cassie drove into town to have lunch with James before going to the hospital.

James was as thrilled as she was and gave her a huge pink teddy for the baby.

'I wish I could come with you, but I've a meeting I can't get out of. Give Mai and Tom my love.'

An unshaven but smiling Tom was waiting for her at the ward entrance.

'Hi, Mum. Come and meet Alice — your granddaughter.'

'Well Done!'

The joy of sailing up the English Channel towards Plymouth Sound at the head of the returning fleet was to be an enduring memory for Lara.

She couldn't believe she'd won the last leg of the race. It was an incredible feeling to know she'd out-sailed some of the best yachtsmen in the world.

Once into Plymouth Sound a stiff breeze had *Clotted Cream* speeding towards the line. Within minutes of the finish gun ringing out, the support boat with Cassie and Tom on board was alongside the yacht and the champagne was flowing.

Tom was the first to clamber on board and Lara sensed the emotion he was feeling as he stepped into the cockpit of his beloved yacht for the first time in months.

'Well done, sis. I'm so proud of you!' he said, giving her a hug.

'Thanks.' Lara hugged him back.

'Congratulations to you, too — Daddy. How are Mai and my new niece?'

'Waiting for you back at the house.'

Cassie was next on board and hugged Lara silently, relieved to have her home safe and sound.

The celebratory cheering that welcomed her into harbour increased the nearer *Clotted Cream* got to her berth. To Lara's amazement there were hundreds of people chanting her name and shouting their good wishes as the yacht was tied up and Lara prepared to go ashore.

Next time she came on board it would be to clear things away, sail the yacht back to the yard and hand her over to Tom. After all they'd been through together, it would be like saying goodbye to an old friend.

Once on the quay crowds of people swarmed around her. Even though she was exhausted, she smiled and waved and tried to sign everything that was thrust at her — pieces of paper, sailing caps, yachting programmes. The world, it seemed, wanted her autograph.

Dexter was waiting for her by the prize-giving table. Oblivious to everybody, he took her in his arms and held her tightly.

'Welcome home, Little Lara. Well done. This is the moment that makes it all worthwhile,' he whispered. 'Enjoy your success.'

There was a discreet cough from the chairman of the race committee. Smiling, Dexter released her to receive her prize and make her acceptance speech.

The winning trophy for this, the last leg, was a glass model of an Open 60s yacht mounted on a polished wooden base. As Lara stood there clutching it tightly, she prayed it wouldn't slip through her shaking hands.

She took a deep breath.

'I can't believe I'm standing here holding this trophy. I have lots of people to thank and, believe me, I do from the bottom of my heart.'

She paused and looked directly at Cassie and Tom.

'I dedicate this trophy to the memory of Miles Lewis, my father.

'I never had the chance to know him properly and I've always missed his presence in my life. But today I truly feel like his daughter and hope he would have been proud of me following in his footsteps.'

In the silence that followed her moving speech, Lara turned away from the microphone and stumbled to Dexter's side. Without a word, he put his arm around her shoulders and handed her a handkerchief to wipe away the tears that were flowing freely down her cheeks.

'Life Is Never Simple'

The sun was streaming in through the window when Cassie awoke on the morning of her wedding day. Tom and Mai had persuaded her to move back to Boatyard House for a couple of days before the wedding and she was glad she'd taken them up on their offer.

She glanced across the room and smiled happily as she saw her outfit hanging on the wardrobe door — a pale cream silk full-length shift dress with a lace coat in a slightly darker shade. It was the most romantic dress Cassie had ever owned.

There was a quiet knock on the door and Lara entered with a breakfast tray.

'Morning, Mum. I thought I'd join you.'

Cassie poured them both a cup of coffee.

'How are all your sponsorship deals working out?' she asked casually.

In the days since she'd been home Lara had been busy sorting out her schedule for the coming months, trying to fit together talks and visits all over the country in a logical sequence so she wouldn't have to repeat journeys too often.

She'd also been trying to fit in meetings with Dexter at least every ten days. It was proving almost impossible.

Lara looked at Cassie.

'Mum, do you think I should give up my solo sailing career before it really begins?' she asked.

Cassie saw the anguish on her daughter's face.

'Lara, love, only you can decide that. But why would you want to? When Sebastian demanded you gave up the race you wouldn't consider it for a minute.'

Lara was silent for a few moments.

'It was different then. I had something to prove. Now . . . ' She shrugged.

'I still love sailing. But there are two problems. One, I'm not sure I'm cut out to be a solo sailor. And two, I think I'll lose any chance of a relationship with Dexter if I start spending week after week at sea.'

'How important is Dexter to you?'

'Very — I think!' Lara smiled.

Cassie took a sip of her coffee.

'Life is never simple, is it?' she said. 'You think you're getting exactly what you want and then something unexpected happens and everything changes. All I can say is, there are always compromises available if you search hard enough. But I do think you will eventually have to decide who or what you cannot live without.'

'Is that what you did when you met Dad?'

Cassie nodded.

'Can I ask you something, Mum?' Lara hesitated before going on. 'Do you love James as much as you loved Dad?'

Cassie looked at her daughter, not wanting to hurt her, but knowing she had to tell the truth.

'Yes. I finally realised I do. But your dad will always have a special place in my heart.'

Cassie went across to the dressing-table and opened her jewellery box. Taking out her old wedding ring, she held it out to Lara.

'Lara, would you like this? I know one day you'll have a wedding ring of your own, but maybe you'd like to wear this on your right hand? After your speech last week I thought you might appreciate a tangible heirloom from your dad and me. And never doubt that he would be as proud of you as I am.'

Lara slipped the ring on to her finger and Cassie took a deep breath.

'I think we'd better start getting ready. Otherwise I'm going to be late for my wedding.'

'The bride's prerogative!' Lara laughed and took the breakfast tray away.

Two hours later, Lara looked at Cassie.

'Mum, you're beautiful. And your outfit is perfect. Right, the cars are here. Gran and I are off to church with Tom and Mai and Alice. Gramps is waiting for you downstairs.'

Half an hour later, standing in the church porch as Lara handed her the bouquet, Cassie glanced into the chapel. James was waiting by the altar, his back towards her.

As though he sensed her watching, he slowly turned and smiled at her. Cassie felt the now familiar lurch of her heart as she smiled back.

'Ready, Cassie?' Bill asked, taking her arm.

Cassie nodded. Yes, she was finally ready to make her way down the aisle towards the man she loved.

As Lara took her place behind her, Cassie couldn't help glancing at her and wondering, in the midst of her own happiness, which path her daughter was going to choose — career woman or wife?

Kisses

Three days after Cassie and James left on their honeymoon, Anna drove Lara to Plymouth to collect *Clotted Cream*. Lara had been hoping that Dexter would be able to join her, but the night before, he'd phoned to tell her he couldn't make it.

Anna turned the car on to the main road.

'Do you have any idea where James has taken Cassie?' she asked.

'A place called Udaipur in north-west India. Mum rang to let us know they'd arrived safely and said it's the most amazing place.

'They're staying in a marble palace built so close to the edge of a huge lake it's like being on board a boat when you look out of a window. It's apparently incredibly romantic.'

'It sounds the perfect place for a honeymoon. How long will they be away?'

'A week. They're due back on Sunday,' Lara said.

Anna glanced at her goddaughter.

'And what about you and Dexter? You seemed very happy together at the wedding.'

'Well, we're certainly trying to make a go of things,' Lara replied. 'But even now I'm back on dry land we're still miles apart most of the time.'

She sighed, remembering the last time she and Dexter had seen each other. They'd wandered off together into the secluded rose garden of the stately home where James and Cassie had held their wedding.

She'd gone willingly into Dexter's arms and returned his kisses with a fervour that surprised both of them.

'Oh, Lara, what are we going to do?' Dexter had murmured, holding her close.

Standing in the circle of his arms Lara had looked up at him.

'We simply won't let life drive us apart.' Her tone was defiant.

Now, though, she wasn't so confident. She glanced at Anna.

'Do you believe that absence makes the heart grow fonder? Or do you agree with Dexter it can sound the death knell for relationships?'

Anna took a few moments before answering.

'I think it depends on how strong the relationship is in the first place — and whether not being together all the time suits both parties. It's when resentment creeps in that trouble starts.

'Things have a way of working themselves out,' she added comfortably. 'You just have to decide on your priorities.'

An hour later, Anna dropped Lara on the quay alongside *Clotted Cream*. Climbing back on board the yacht was like returning home.

Everything was so reassuringly familiar. Lara took a deep breath. Oh, it was good to be back on board!

Motoring out of the Sound into the Channel, Lara took an easterly bearing before cutting the engine and starting to hoist the mainsail. She intended to enjoy a final solo sail before handing the boat back to Tom.

Standing at the tiller holding the

yacht on her course up the Channel, Lara tried again to think coherently about her future.

Everybody, including Dexter, kept telling her to do what she wanted. The trouble was she no longer knew what that was.

But as she enjoyed the familiar sensation of *Clotted Cream* riding the waves, Lara realised she couldn't give up her involvement in the yachting world any more than she could give up Dexter.

What was it that Cassie had said about compromise?

An Offer He Couldn't Refuse?

It was the final evening of their honeymoon and Cassie and James were enjoying a romantic moonlit dinner on a raft moored several yards out into the lake.

On shore the floodlit marble palace was reflected in the quietly lapping waters and there was the gentle sound of a sitar drifting out on the breeze towards them.

'Cassie, we have to talk about the future,' James said, filling her glass with champagne.

Cassie looked at him and waited.

'This letter arrived last Saturday as I left for the church. I'd completely forgotten about it until this evening.' James handed Cassie an envelope.

'It's from an old Naval friend congratulating me and . . . well, read it for yourself.'

Cassie quickly scanned the short note.

'It's a year's contract to help run — ' she glanced back down at the letter ' — La Marina des Oiseaux.'

James was watching her anxiously.

'It's right down on the Med, close to the French/Spanish border. I haven't been there for years, but it's a very beautiful part of the world.'

'Do you want this job?' Cassie asked quietly.

'Well, it's the only firm offer I've had since my redundancy. And yes, I do quite like the idea of a year down south, but it's no longer a decision I can take alone. The new Mrs White has a major say now.'

He reached across the table and took hold of her hand.

'Cassie, I only opened the letter two hours ago so I haven't had much time to think about it, either. But it did cross my mind that maybe we could sell my boat, buy a bigger one, sail down there and live on board for a year. Then, when the contract ends, we'd sail back to England. It would be an adventure for our middle years.'

'I thought you'd virtually decided to take early retirement,' Cassie said slowly.

'I still can, but I do feel as though I've been thrown on the scrapheap too soon at the moment,' James said, his tone thoughtful.

There was a short silence before Cassie replied.

'Well, it would certainly be a completely new start to our married life together. It's a long time since I lived on board a boat but, like you say, it would be an adventure to remember together.'

She picked up her wine glass and took a sip, hoping James wouldn't notice her hand shaking. She re-read the letter.

'Your friend says the contract would start in a couple of months. That doesn't give us much time to organise everything.'

She did a quick calculation of dates.

'It would mean leaving immediately after Alice's christening.'

Cassie took a deep breath.

'OK. You'd better tell your friend you'd like the job. Tell him, too, Mr and Mrs White would like a berth reserved in the marina for their as yet unpurchased floating home.'

Dexter's Project

Lara found the whole experience of recording a radio programme intriguing and exciting. To her surprise her initial nervousness soon disappeared and she thoroughly enjoyed talking about her round-the-world experiences.

Suzie, the producer, switched her microphone off at the end.

'Thanks, Lara. That was great. You're a natural. Will you come back at the end of the month and take part in a discussion with some teenagers? The schools around here followed your trip and I know some of the girls look on you as a role model.'

'Gosh, that's scary,' Lara said. 'I'd love to, if I can fit it in. Let's take a look in the diary.'

Half an hour later, having agreed to do another two programmes, Lara set off for Dexter's family farm.

Not far from the north Somerset coast, the farm sat at the end of a long track with woods behind it. In the distance across the fields the occasional glint of the Bristol Channel could be seen.

After coffee in the farmhouse kitchen with his parents, Dexter found her a pair of wellingtons and took her on a tour.

When they returned he stopped in front of some outbuildings on the edge of the yard.

'Well, apart from my surprise in here, I think you've seen everything Home Farm has to offer.'

The building Dexter had stopped in front of had large double doors. He lifted up the closing bar and swung the doors open.

Inside, shored up with lengths of timber, was a forty-foot fibreglass sailing boat.

'I bought it with the proceeds from my flat in the States. I thought in the dim and distant future you and I would enjoy sailing her together,' Dexter said.

'She only arrived two days ago. The hull is basically OK but the interior needs a lot of work.' He looked at Lara.

'It's my project to keep me out of mischief while you're busy sailing the seven seas. Hopefully it will stop me missing you too much.'

Lara was quiet for a moment as she walked around the hull.

'Lovely lines. She should be quite fast. Can we go on board?'

'There's a ladder around the other side. I'll give you a hand up.'

Sitting next to Dexter on one of the bunks in the cabin, Lara spoke.

'I've been thinking about missing you, too. And I've decided to do something about it. But first I need to ask you something.'

'Ask away,' he said, giving her a hug.

'You know how you helped me with taking over *Clotted Cream* after Tom's accident, sorting out the media business and recently drumming up sponsors for me?

'Well, I was going to ask if you'd continue to do that, be my manager, if you like.

'But now you've got the boat as a project, you're going to be busier than ever . . . ' Her voice trailed away.

Dexter pulled her closer.

'Lara, I'd love to be your manager. The farm has to be my main priority for the next few months, but I'll definitely be able to help you. There's no time limit on restoring the boat.'

'Thank you.' Lara smiled happily. 'Now the other thing is, I've got to find somewhere to live. I know I can still stay at Boatyard House, but Tom and Mai would probably appreciate having the place to themselves. I was thinking I might move nearer here — Bath or Bristol, maybe.'

'We'll have a look in the local paper later to see what's available for rent. You really have been thinking about things, haven't you?'

'Yep. There's something else, too, but until it's finalised I'm not telling you what it is. By the way, I'm going up to London next week to see the sponsors.'

'Do you want your new manager to

come with you?' Dexter asked.

Lara shook her head.

'Not on this occasion, thanks.

'Now, tell me your plans for the yacht.' She deliberately changed the topic of conversation before Dexter could ask for details about her meeting with the sponsors.

Lucky

The weeks leading up to the christening passed in a blur of activity for everyone.

The whole family greeted the news that Cassie and James were to live in France for a year with enthusiasm.

'Good for James,' Tom said. 'We'll definitely be down to see you both.'

Lara had hugged her.

'It'll be great, Mum — all that sunshine. I'll be visiting, too.'

Bill and Liz were quieter in their good wishes.

'I'll miss you,' her mother said, holding Cassie tightly. 'Are you sure it's only for a year?'

Only for a year or not, there was a lot of organising to do. One of the first things Cassie and James discussed was what to do with Solo.

'There's no problem with the quarantine laws these days, so she can always come with us,' James said. 'She'd soon get used to the boat.'

But Cassie was doubtful. She felt Solo would be happier staying on land. Bill said he'd be pleased to keep her down in the yard.

'She's a good guard dog, that one.'

But Cassie couldn't bear the thought of Solo being in a kennel on cold winter nights.

Solo solved the problem herself by disappearing from River View Cottage one afternoon while Cassie and James were busy packing. When a distraught Cassie finally tracked her down she was asleep in the small garden of Boatyard House.

Mai had put Alice outside in her pram and Solo had taken up position alongside.

'She really took to Alice while you were away. She's very protective towards her. We'd love to have her — not just while you're away, but permanently,' Mai said. 'If that's possible?'

'That would be wonderful,' Cassie said. 'I was worried about leaving her but I know she'll be happy with you.'

Bill had agreed to sell them River View Cottage and there was all the legal side of the purchase to be seen to before they left.

Then there was the question of finding a suitable boat for the trip down to the Mediterranean. Days were spent looking through sales brochures and scouring the yachting press.

Finally, two weeks before they were due to leave, they found the perfect vessel.

Moored in Fowey, it was a forty-two-foot motor sailer, more than capable of coping with the trip down south. The good news as far as James and Cassie were concerned was that she was in a totally seaworthy condition.

When they looked her over they couldn't believe how lucky they'd been to find her. Cassie had smiled when she'd first seen the name *My Dream*. It couldn't have been more appropriate.

She and James motored her back and moored her on one of the boatyard pontoons. Now *My Dream* was anchored outside River View Cottage, being loaded up for the voyage.

'New Contract'

With just a week to go before the christening, Lara was on her way to see Dexter. She'd had news about her sponsorship and wanted to tell him face to face. She phoned from a service station on the outskirts of Weston to let him know she was coming.

'Nothing's wrong, is it?' he asked worriedly. 'You're all right?'

'I'm fine. I'll see you soon.'

Dexter was waiting for her at the top of the farm drive. As she stopped the car he peered anxiously through the car window.

'Shall we go for a walk?' she suggested.

Taking her hand, he led her in the direction of a small wood in the distance.

'Right, Lara, what's this all about?'

'I've had a phone call from the sponsors. There's a new contract for me in the post. Actually it's on its way to you for checking and final approval.'

Dexter waited.

'You'll notice a few adjustments when it gets here and I wanted to tell you about them myself.' Lara took a deep breath.

'The last few weeks have been really difficult, trying to decide what to do. I love you. I love sailing. I couldn't bear the thought of not being with you, but I also couldn't bear the thought of not sailing competitively any more.

'So, I've taken Mum's advice and

compromised. I've decided not to do any more races like the Around Alone or the next Vendée Globe.' She glanced at Dexter, trying to judge his reaction, but his face was expressionless as he waited for her to continue.

'Instead I'm going to concentrate on shorter races like the Route du Rhum and the Mini Transat. I'll still be away at times but it won't be for months on end.

'I'm also going to try to increase my media work. Suzie at the local radio station up here is keen for me to present a sporting quiz programme.

'I've still got my book to write and there are lots of talks lined up for the next few months.'

'Why didn't you tell me what you were trying to do?' Dexter asked.

'I thought you might say I was silly not accepting such a fantastic offer. Besides I wasn't sure whether the sponsors would agree to altering the contract.'

Dexter was silent for a moment or two.

'It's wonderful news, Lara. I'm really pleased it's all working out,' he said eventually.

'But what?' Lara said. 'I can definitely sense a 'but'.'

'I just wish you hadn't made all these decisions behind my back. I know you meant well, Lara, but if we're going to have any sort of future together we must talk to each other. No secrets about anything. Promise?'

'I promise. Am I forgiven?' she asked quietly.

By way of an answer Dexter pulled her into his arms.

'It's going to be fantastic to have the time to get to know each other properly,' he said.

And then he kissed her.

'Our Time'

The day of the christening dawned bright and clear. Cassie gazed out of the window of River View Cottage at

My Dream gently bobbing up and down on her anchor. Tonight, she and James planned to sleep on board, ready for a dawn start tomorrow on the early high tide.

Cassie suppressed a sigh. James was so enthusiastic about his new job that most of the time he carried her along with him. It was only when she was on her own that she grew apprehensive.

Although she was looking forward to the year ahead, a tiny part of her was afraid they were doing the wrong thing.

As though sensing her thoughts, James appeared in the kitchen and put his arm around her.

'Morning, Cassie. Penny for them?'

Cassie shook her head. She couldn't bring herself to voice her worries, but of course, James realised she was concerned about their decision.

'Cassie, my love,' James began, holding her close, 'I know it's a big step we're taking but it will be all right, you'll see. It's only natural for you to miss the family, but you and I will be together. This is our time. And I promise you, Cassie, come what may, I'll always be there for you.'

Cassie smiled at him. What he said was true. Her life was with James now. She had to learn to let go.

She stood on tiptoe and kissed him.

'I know, James. Once we've set sail tomorrow morning everything will fall in place and I'll be fine.'

Later that afternoon, standing in the tiny country church where Tom and Mai had decided to have Alice christened, Cassie looked around at her family gathered together in front of the fifteenth-century font.

Lara was carefully holding Alice, who looked beautiful in the antique christening gown that generations of Lewis children had been christened in. Dexter at her side looked nervous. Would their wedding be the next time the whole family was together again in church? Cassie could only hope.

Tom and Mai, the proud parents, stood alongside, listening as the godparents made their promises. Bill and Liz, now proud great-grandparents, were standing behind the vicar with happy smiles on their faces.

The vicar had given permission for James to take photographs of the ceremony. Now, as he raised his camera, he smiled at Cassie before he pressed the button and took a picture of the whole Lewis family that was to become one of Cassie's most treasured possessions over the months to come.

'Bon Voyage'

At 5.30 the next morning *My Dream* slipped her anchor and slowly began to make her way down river to the Channel and then on to the open sea.

As they motored past the boatyard Cassie saw a light on and knew that her father was watching them leave. She raised her arm in acknowledgement, hoping that Bill could see her final goodbye in the breaking dawn.

Bill, drinking his early morning tea in his customary place in the workshop, saw the wave and raised his own hand in farewell as the boat motored past.

'*Bon voyage*, Cassie and James. Come back safe.'

THE END

We do hope that you have enjoyed reading this large print book.

Did you know that all of our titles are available for purchase?

We publish a wide range of high quality large print books including:
Romances, Mysteries, Classics
General Fiction
Non Fiction and Westerns

Special interest titles available in large print are:
The Little Oxford Dictionary
Music Book, Song Book
Hymn Book, Service Book

Also available from us courtesy of Oxford University Press:
Young Readers' Dictionary
(large print edition)
Young Readers' Thesaurus
(large print edition)

For further information or a free brochure, please contact us at:
Ulverscroft Large Print Books Ltd.,
The Green, Bradgate Road, Anstey,
Leicester, LE7 7FU, England.
Tel: (00 44) **0116 236 4325**
Fax: (00 44) **0116 234 0205**

FATEFUL DECEPTION

Kate Allan

When Captain Robert Monceaux, of the Fifteenth Light Dragoons, rescues Miss Lucinda Handscombe from a highway robbery, she piques his interest. Robert cannot stay away from her, and Lucinda becomes attracted to him. When her guardian demands that she accompanies him to Madeira against her will, Robert offers to save her. But, after a misunderstanding, Lucinda runs away. And when Robert eventually finds her, they realise they must learn to trust each other for their future happiness together.

GROWING DREAMS

Chrissie Loveday

After the death of her long-absent ex-husband, Samantha Rayner and her young daughter Allie move to Pengelly in Cornwall to start afresh. When they stumble across the overgrown grounds of Pengelly Hall, Sam starts dreaming of restoring them to their former glory. Jackson Clark, the business-minded owner of Pengelly Hall, agrees to fund the project, but could Sam have taken on more than she bargained for . . . And what secrets does head gardener Will Heston hold in his past?

MAIL ORDER BRIDE

Catriona McCuaig

Lydia McFarlane has been used to a life of wealth and privilege, but when her father remarries, her new stepmother starts a systematic campaign to remove Lydia from the family home in Ontario, plotting to marry her off to a man who doesn't love her. Lydia decides to take matters into her own hands, and runs away to the prairie town of Alberta to become a mail order bride — but life in the Golden West is not as idyllic as Lydia has imagined . . .

SILVERSTRAND

Diney Delancey

Working for the Distress Call Agency, Tara Dereham travels from London to the seaside town of Silverstrand, to help Mrs Ward run her guesthouse. But when Mrs Ward falls ill, Tara has to manage the business and care for her client's grandson, helped by one of the guests, Steven Harris. But there is a secret in the Ward family, and danger looms for Tara as she learns more of the secret and of the people concerned.

FOREVER AUTUMN

Christina Jones

After a heartbreaking deception, Stephanie Gibson decides to change her life completely. She moves to the south coast to work as a nanny for the large and scatty Matthews family. Her employers are friendly and eccentric, and Stephanie soon settles in. She is enchanted by her charge, Nikki, and loves the challenge of her new job. However, when she finds herself falling in love again, spectres from the past loom up. Has Stephanie made another mistake and will she ever learn to trust again?